A LOYAL HEART

Books by Jody Hedlund

Young Adult
The Vow: Prequel Novella
An Uncertain Choice
A Daring Sacrifice
For Love & Honor

The Orphan Train Series
An Awakened Heart: A Novella
With You Always
Together Forever

The Beacons of Hope Series
Out of the Storm: A Novella
Love Unexpected
Hearts Made Whole
Undaunted Hope
Forever Safe
Never Forget

The Hearts of Faith Collection
The Preacher's Bride
The Doctor's Lady
Rebellious Heart

The Michigan Brides Collection
Unending Devotion
A Noble Groom
Captured by Love

Historical
Luther and Katharina
Newton & Polly

A LOYAL HEART

JODY HEDLUND

NORTHERN LIGHTS PRESS

A Loyal Heart
Northern Lights Press
© 2018 Copyright
Jody Hedlund Print Edition

www.jodyhedlund.com

ISBN: 978-0-692-05523-6

Scripture quotations are taken from the King James Version of the Bible.

This is a work of historical reconstruction; the appearances of certain historical figures are accordingly inevitable. All other characters are products of the author's imagination. Any resemblance to actual events or locales or persons, living or dead, is entirely coincidental.

Cover Design by Emilie Hendryx of E.A. Hendryx Creative

Chapter
1

Ludlow Castle, Eastern Marches
June, in the year of our Lord 1392

"The inner bailey wall to the south is down, my lady, and the castle will soon be overrun." The soldier faltered in the doorway of my chambers, his armor slick with the blood of battle.

The news of the collapse didn't surprise me. After all, I'd spent the past night, like everyone else, anxiously listening to the steady ring of picks as sappers chipped away the last of the stone under the wall. From the moment Lord Pitt's sappers started digging the underground passageway beneath the walled fortifications several days ago, I'd known it was only a matter of time before they broke into the castle. I just never expected it to be so quickly.

While I'd hoped the tunnel would weaken

and collapse on the sappers in order to halt their progress, they'd moved with remarkable speed and without any mishaps, clearly well commanded. I'd ordered my captain of the guard to do whatever he could to stop the digging, but he'd been too busy fending off siege engines and invaders scaling the walls.

The soldier's knees began to buckle, but he grabbed onto the doorframe to hold himself erect. Only then did I see the trail of crimson running from between his gorget around his neck and his pauldron.

I yanked at the top sheet of my bed, made a slit with my sword, and ripped off a piece of linen. "You are losing too much blood," I said, crossing to the soldier. "Stuff this under your armor against the wound to staunch the flow."

My own shoulder piece flapped as I pressed the material into the defenseless spot of the soldier's armor. Cecil had begun helping me don my armor the moment I received word the sappers had dragged brush and a fatty hog carcass into their underground passageway. A short while later, I watched out my high window as a torch man crawled inside to light the brush and hog. He'd barely made it out before the explosion rocked the castle.

My padding and chain mail were in place. But Cecil had only managed to assemble half my armor—the cuisse covering my thighs along with my breastplate and pauldrons. Now, we had no time to finish.

"You can't tend the wounded, Olivia," Cecil admonished. His slender face with his pointed black goatee radiated with rare urgency. "You need to escape through the west exit. Now. While Lord Pitt's soldiers are distracted in the throes of battle."

Though I'd planned to join the fighting to defend the keep, Cecil was right. This might be my only chance to sneak my sister away. I nodded curtly and stalked to my helmet where it lay on the end of my bed. "We shall disguise Izzy as one of the servants."

Cecil bowed his head, revealing the shiny bald circle surrounded by thinning black hair. With bronzed skin, his Moorish ancestry was difficult to ignore. But his diminutive stature as well as gnarled limbs disguised the threat of his strength and cunning.

To anyone else, Cecil appeared to be nothing more than an old, crippled slave. But he was not only my personal trainer. He was my fiercest protector, my wisest advisor, and my most trusted friend.

He was the only one who could address me, the Earl of Ulster's daughter, without my title of Lady Olivia. No one else dared such informality.

Tucking my helmet under my arm, I grabbed my weapon belt which contained the sword

Cecil had crafted especially for me, lightweight yet powerful. I didn't have time for the gauntlets for my hands or the sabatons to cover my leather boots.

"Return to the captain," I said to the soldier waiting in the doorway. "Instruct him to distract the enemy in the inner bailey and hold them off as long as possible so that I might take Lady Isabelle to safety."

He bowed his subservience before spinning and stumbling back the same direction he'd come, his armor clanking with each labored step.

I would need every second the knights could give me. As if sensing the same, Cecil was already hobbling across my chamber to the boudoir that led to the inner door connecting my chambers to Izzy's.

As I entered the private room I used for bathing and dressing, I inhaled the sweetness of lavender and roses scattered among my many garments to keep them from taking on the scent of the damp and musty castle walls.

I followed Cecil past the massive walnut armoire and matching dressing table and past the locked chest that held all my jewelry. Did I have time to take a few of the most precious items? Perhaps the jewels that had belonged to my mother—the only links I had left to the gentle and kind woman who had died shortly after Izzy's birth nearly fifteen years ago, when I'd been only three.

Father had married twice thereafter. His second wife had borne him a long-coveted son but she died a year later. His childless third wife, the current Countess of Ulster, had mothered Charles as if he were her own.

The countess was cold and formal and treated Izzy and me like foreign guests. In spite of her lack of warmth, I did appreciate her devotion to my half-brother, especially because at six years of age, he was sickly and in need of constant attention which she willingly gave him. At least they were safe at Wigmore Castle, my father's principal seat of residence.

"My mother's jewels," I called to Cecil, stopping next to the chest. "I shall take the most precious."

Cecil shook his head as I'd suspected he would. "We don't have time."

I pictured several pieces of my mother's jewels. My favorite was the circular gold brooch studded with emeralds, the one my mother had often worn to pin her cloak closed. She'd told me the vibrant green was the same shade as my eyes and just as beautiful, the only aspect of my appearance I'd inherited from her.

Everything else about me resembled Father—my determined temperament, red hair, fair skin, and striking features. Still, my numerous suitors would have vied for me even if I'd been as ugly as a mule. Along with my father's wealth and land, he was one of the most powerful magnates of the Marches which made me a prized catch among the nobility.

During the past year of playing the courtship game, I'd known as well as Father where my future lay.

With Lionel Lacy.

Ahead, Cecil was entering Izzy's chambers and calling sharp instructions to her maidservant. My attention dropped to my jewelry chest again. At the very least, I should save the bracelet Lionel had recently given me.

The Lacys were another powerful Marcher family. Uniting the families in marriage would strengthen Father's power and wealth. During Father's last visit to Ludlow, he'd confided in me that he was making arrangements with the Marquess of Clearwater for my betrothal to Lionel.

As the oldest son, Lionel would one day inherit his father's title of marquess as well as his wealth and holdings. Through the marriage, I would gain a new status as the future March-ioness of Clearwater, would spend time at the king's court, and would likely become one of the queen's ladies-in-waiting. I'd be in a place to hear valuable information as well as influence the other ladies, maybe even the queen herself.

Such connections would put me in a position to help my father in any way he needed and show him my worth as a daughter.

Certainly Father would want me to save as many of our valuable jewels as possible. Moreover, it would only take an extra minute to retrieve the chest key from its hiding place. I spun on my heels and returned to my chambers, ignoring the slapping footsteps and shouts in the hallway.

Father would be sorely disappointed when he learned I'd allowed Ludlow Castle to fall to Lord Pitt, one of his grievous, longtime enemies. I'd been able to send Father a quickly scrawled note just before Lord Pitt's troops had arrived and laid siege to the castle. For the past week, I'd prayed he received my note and would make haste to aid me with his army of retainers.

However, my hopes had dwindled with each passing day, especially as Lord Pitt's men relentlessly broke down our defenses.

I crossed to the corner, knelt, and began brushing away the rushes to reveal the wood planks underneath. My fingers made quick work of prying up the loose board and finding the key underneath.

The battle cries and clamor stealing in the open window seemed louder, almost as if they were coming from inside the castle now. I had to hurry or we might lose our chance to escape.

Without bothering to replace the board, I returned to the boudoir and knelt in front of the chest. Before I could wiggle the key into the lock, Cecil reappeared dragging Izzy with him. She clutched her gown closed where apparently the servant had been in the process of unlacing it. Izzy's light blue eyes were wild with fright, and her blond hair a disheveled tangle under the servant's head covering.

"They're here," Cecil hissed. "Hide in the armoires."

Without a moment's hesitation, I grabbed Izzy and swung open the heavy armoire door. Out of the corner of my eye, I saw Cecil shuffle into my chambers.

I wanted to shout after him to find a place to hide too. I didn't want him to take any risks with the invading army. But such admonitions would go unheeded. Cecil was more stubborn than I was. I'd have to trust he'd find a way to keep himself safe. Although he was no longer the young Moorish warrior he'd once been, he was still skilled beyond most.

"Climb behind the gowns." I shoved Izzy into the heavy garments.

She whimpered, her skin ashen. My sister contained everything good and fair in this world and was like our mother in every way that I was not.

"Do not make a sound and do not come out,"

I ordered as I closed the door. "Not for any reason."

The bang of my chamber door and clanking footfalls was followed by shouts.

Without further thought, I yanked my helmet over my head and unsheathed my sword. I had no time to climb into the armoire opposite Izzy's. Instead, I sidled next to it into the dark shadows of the windowless room. If anyone peeked into the boudoir, I'd be mostly out of sight.

And if they came into the small dressing room to search more thoroughly, I'd slit their throats before they had the chance to discover Izzy's hiding place.

"Where are they?" came a sharp voice from my chamber.

The heavy footsteps on the rushes told me there were several soldiers searching the room. I was surprised they'd infiltrated the castle and found my chambers so rapidly. Whoever was leading the campaign was obviously informed and efficient. Even if I was in great danger, I could still appreciate a well-executed attack.

"The Earl of Ulster's daughters have already made their escape," Cecil said with the slight accent of his native language.

A moment of silence ensued, and I could envision the intruders scanning the room and seeing signs of my recent presence. I closed my eyes and prayed they wouldn't notice the remains of my morning meal on the bedside table.

"Continue to search," the sharp voice finally barked. "Check everywhere. Leave no door unopened."

The footsteps resumed and began to cross to the boudoir.

I slid my fingers more securely around the hilt of my sword. The handle was perfectly shaped to fit my slender fingers. And thanks to Cecil's drills, I could wield it as expertly as any knight. The only problem was that I'd never fought in a real battle, and my breath hitched slightly at the prospect of taking up my weapon with the intent to cause bodily injury.

"The earl's daughters left earlier this morning." Cecil spoke more adamantly.

I didn't have to be in the room to know he was reaching for the knife hidden at the small of his back. My lungs constricted at the realization that Cecil would fight to the death to keep the knights from entering the boudoir and discovering our presence.

At one time Cecil may have had the capability of defending himself against overwhelming odds. But not anymore. He'd put up a vicious fight, but he wouldn't be able to single-handedly defeat this group.

I wouldn't stand idly by while he sacrificed

his life. I didn't care if he raged at me later for disobeying his instructions. I could do nothing less than come to his aid.

The moment the knight advancing toward the boudoir gave a cry of pain, I sprang from my hiding spot. The clank of metal against metal told me Cecil had unsheathed his sword an instant after throwing his knife. He'd injured one and was now engaged in combat.

As I careened into my bedchamber, my pulse stuttered for an instant at the realization that I was about to enter combat. But as my sights connected with Cecil dodging one sword while slashing at two others, my ire and frustration shoved aside the nervousness.

I sprang at the broader and taller of the knights who had his back to me and angled my sword toward the unprotected spot at the joints of the armor—the slit in his cuisse.

My sword jabbed into his upper thigh, but before I could thrust it deep, the knight spun and his blade came down on my gauntlet with such force that I jerked away and retreated several steps. I fumbled with my weapon and almost dropped it.

In the meantime, the knight brought his sword around in an arc toward my unprotected lower legs.

If not for the quick reflexes Cecil had drilled into me, my opponent would have severed my limbs. As it was, I jumped in the air tucking my legs underneath my body, more nimble than usual since I was only wearing half my armor. The knight's blade slashed at air, but just as rapidly came back around aiming at my unprotected neck.

I leapt onto my bed, grateful the thick curtains had been pulled aside. I balanced on the bed frame and deflected the blow intended to slice open my jugular vein. Then I passed forward and aimed for his armpit.

He pivoted before I could connect, and my sword clanked across his gardbrace. I prepared to shed his next move so I could again attack one of the weak spots in his armor. But as he spun to face me, he paused.

Through the slits in his helmet, dark midnight blue eyes studied me. In a sweeping glance, he took me in from my helmet to my unprotected hands and down to my slim fitting leather boots.

Behind him, Cecil fought the other two as nimbly as a man half his age. But I could see he was tiring, which meant I had to do something to end this skirmish.

Once more, I swung my sword at my opponent, hoping this time to catch him off guard. Instead of parrying with me, he ducked and then grabbed the wrist of my fighting hand. He twisted with such force that an involuntary cry escaped me. I had no choice but to drop my weapon. In the same instant, he jerked me off the bed.

I stumbled to the floor and lunged for my sword. But as I bent, he wrapped his thick arm around my neck and brought me up in a headlock. His grip was so tight at my neck I could hardly breathe. Even so, I slipped my hand to the dagger I wore strapped to my side underneath my chain mail.

In an instant, I had my knife out and jabbed it backward, hoping my aim was correct and that the blade would plunge into the narrow breathing space in his helmet and sink into his neck.

But the knight had quicker reflexes than even Cecil. Before I knew what was happening, he'd disarmed me and pressed my knife against my throat.

The blade bit my skin in the first nip of death.

Chapter 2

I PRESSED THE YOUNG KNIGHT'S DAGGER AGAINST HIS throat, only enough to scare him into compliance. I had no intention of killing a boy—even if he was well-trained.

"Stop!" the Moor cried, backing away from his opponents, his attention fixed upon the blade at the boy's throat. "We surrender!"

The fright in the dark-skinned man's eyes told me more than words. This boy I had within my grasp was someone of importance, someone the Moor had been willing to defend to the death.

"Cease your fighting," I commanded my men.

They complied and dropped their swords to their sides but without taking their attention from the Moor. I had no doubt he would have killed my knights if he'd been given the chance to fight them long enough. Already one was wounded and favoring his non-fighting arm.

The boy squirmed against me, and I loosened the knife at his throat, not wishing to cause him more harm. He wasn't seasoned. The slender fingers, clean fingernails, and unblemished skin told me he hadn't been in battle before.

Who was he?

Before surrounding Ludlow Castle, my sources had informed me the earl's daughters were inside but that his young son lived at one of his other residences.

Had my sources been wrong about the son? Was this the earl's heir after all? I'd assumed he was but a young child. Had I misinterpreted the information?

The Moor's eyes glittered with a determination that warned me not to trust him. He'd lash out and kill all three of us as soon as he could manage it.

"Bind the Moor," I ordered.

He started to resist.

I tightened the dagger against my prisoner's throat. The young man released a cry of pain—a very unmanly cry. But the cry—as I'd suspected— was all it took to make the Moor submit. His easy acquiescence only confirmed the importance of my captive.

I waited patiently as my men used the cord from the bed curtain to fasten the Moor's arms behind his back. Even then, I wasn't sure the man was contained. "Tie him to the chair."

As my men worked to further secure the Moor,

the knights I'd sent to explore the other chambers in the living quarters returned. They were empty-handed. "No sign of the daughters, Sir Aldric."

I'd sensed the Moor had been lying when he'd claimed that the earl's daughters had escaped. But what if my instincts were wrong? It would be a first.

And if I failed this mission, it would also be a first. During the year I'd been working for Lord Pitt, I hadn't failed a single mission. In fact, I'd been so successful Pitt had made me captain of his army.

More importantly, he'd finally offered me forgiveness for my debt and the grievances against him. I'd long since repaid him two times the amount I'd owed. I'd also long since reimbursed the other lords. My gambling debts were gone. And I'd even managed to replenish Maidstone's coffers. Although my brother Bennet and his wife Sabine hadn't wanted my repayment for the sacrifices they'd made for me, they hadn't been able to turn down my occasional gifts—the relics and artwork I gleaned on my raids.

Already in my short time within Ludlow Castle, I'd noted that the keep contained a wealth of treasures sure to please Pitt. As always, he'd pay me for my service to him by giving me a portion of the spoils. However, this time, Pitt had entrusted me not only with bringing him the wealth inside the castle but with capturing the earl's children.

If the mission hadn't come down from the king himself, I likely wouldn't have agreed to command the troops. It was one thing to lead raids against criminals and rogues and rebels of the crown. It was another thing entirely to involve families, particularly innocent children. Even if Pitt and the king had good reason to take the earl's daughters, I wasn't fully convinced their plan was justified.

Whatever the case, I'd committed myself and now would see the mission through to completion. That meant finding the earl's daughters and delivering them to Pitt.

I studied the Moor a moment longer, his face now impassive and giving nothing away. This young man within my grasp was the key in getting the Moor to divulge his secrets. Without releasing the knife's pressure at the boy's throat, I grabbed one of his slender hands and held it up.

"I will give you to the count of five to tell me where the earl's daughters really are, or I'll start cutting off this boy's fingers." My tone was rigid and uncompromising. I wouldn't cut off his fingers, but they didn't know that.

"One, two, three . . ."

The Moor made eye contact with the boy who shook his head, as if in warning. Apparently he and the Moor were working together at hiding the daughters.

"Four, five." I flipped the knife from the boy's throat to his hand and pressed the knife against his thumb.

"Wait!" came a girl's voice behind me.

I glanced over my shoulder to see a pale-faced young girl stumble out of a side door. Her blue eyes were frightened, her golden hair in disarray, and her bodice askew as though she'd begun to change but hadn't finished.

At the same moment, I could sense the change in posture of my captive, the slow sag in his shoulders and the draining of his resistance.

"Please don't hurt her." The girl's voice trembled and tears streaked her cheeks.

Her?

I spun my prisoner and wrenched the helmet away, revealing a woman's beautiful face with high cheekbones, an elegant nose, and full lips. Although her red hair was pulled back into a messy knot, strands had come loose and framed her smooth, unblemished skin. If she wasn't already stunning enough, her brilliant green eyes framed by long dark lashes made her more so.

Eyes that peered at me with contempt.

As a wave of self-loathing washed over me, I slackened my hold on her. I'd fought against a lady, pressed a knife to her throat, and threatened to cut off her thumb. Only the worst kind of brutes engaged in such treatment of women, and I didn't consider myself to be one of them. No matter how low I'd once sunk into gambling and drinking, I'd always treated women with the respect they were due. And that hadn't changed.

"I beg your forgiveness, my lady." I released her and tossed her dagger to the bed. "I didn't realize you were a woman or I wouldn't have—"

In an instant, she scooped her sword from the floor and pressed the tip into the slit in my gorget against my neck. Her lovely chin rose a notch, and her green eyes glinted with anger. "Tell your men to release my servant. Let him take my sister away, and I shall hand myself over to you."

"No, Olivia," the young blond-haired woman said, shaking her head frantically.

Olivia Norfolk. The eldest daughter of the Earl of Ulster. From her beauty, I should have guessed her identity. I'd overheard other noblemen speak about the earl's strikingly beautiful daughters, but I hadn't expected Olivia to be quite so vibrant, so alive, so exquisite.

I found myself unable to move, unable to do anything except stare at her. It was quite clear her beauty had the capability of casting a spell upon men, rendering them into marble sculptures.

"Go now, Izzy," Olivia said to the other woman, who was decidedly younger, most likely the earl's other daughter, Isabelle Norfolk.

Now that I'd discovered who I was looking for, doubts rose to assail me. I couldn't take these two innocent women as prisoners back to Pitt, could I? They weren't a part of the earl's schemes, and they surely didn't deserve to suffer for their father's evil plots.

Maybe if I let them escape, I could find a viable excuse to give Pitt regarding my failed mission.

Just as soon as the thought came, I let it pass. The Earl of Ulster was stirring up dissension against the king. Already the Marcher barons resisted submitting to the king, often refusing to pay taxes and follow his laws. As one of the strongest leaders, the earl was attempting to strengthen alliances among the border lords as well as the Welsh. Everyone knew such alliances would only end in outright war against the king.

But if we stopped the earl now and forced him into compliance with the king, we would weaken the alliances and set an example for all the other Marcher barons. I'd agreed with Pitt and the king that taking the earl's daughters as prisoners and holding them for ransom would force the earl to submit. I couldn't throw away the plans now.

"Make haste, Izzy." Olivia's voice turned urgent, and her sister's eyes widened, flickering back and forth between Olivia and the Moor who was still bound securely in the chair.

As if sensing that her sister was too frightened to go anywhere on her own, Olivia thrust the tip of her sword further into my gorget and motioned to my men. "Let Cecil go this instant, or I shall kill your commander."

The knights hurried toward the Moor.

I sighed at their lack of confidence in my abilities. After watching me fight these many months, surely they knew I wouldn't succumb so easily.

I jerked backward, breaking the connection with Olivia's sword. At the same time I brought my forearm up with enough power to knock the weapon from her grip. It flew into the air. I caught it then spun and pointed the blade against the Moor's chest.

The man didn't flinch, not even to blink.

In addition to having a weak spot for her sister, Olivia had one for this servant. She'd given away as much in the few minutes I'd observed her. Concern for him had likely brought her out of the boudoir in the first place. Now I would use that knowledge against her.

"My lady." I adjusted the hilt and tested the light weight, guessing the sword had been handcrafted just for her. She had some skill with her weapon, had been trained well. But no matter her abilities, I was stronger, more experienced, and more capable. She'd never be able to outfight or outwit me. She needed to know the battle was over and that she must surrender graciously or it wouldn't go well for her.

"I am under orders to deliver you and your sister to Lord Pitt alive." I moved the sharp blade of her sword near the Moor's face. "If you cooperate, I shall spare your servants any ill will."

I lifted my gaze to hers, to those startlingly green eyes that now glittered with haughty anger.

"But if you fail to submit to my command, you'll force me to find less pleasant ways to do my job." Without breaking my gaze from hers, I sliced off the tip of the Moor's pointed goatee so that black wiry hair drifted to his lap.

Her attention flickered to her servant, a shadow of anxiety flitting across her features. Yet even with her concern for the man she'd called Cecil, she jutted her chin stubbornly. "Take me, but leave my sister."

Keeping a hard, unrelenting glare upon Olivia, I sliced the servant's goatee again, this time purposefully grazing his chin.

She winced at the sight of the blood I'd drawn. I knew without looking the wound was only skin deep, but I hoped it was enough to scare her.

For several taut moments, she held the gaze of her servant, silent communication passing between them, in which I guessed he was admonishing her to comply. At least for now. Not because he feared for his own life or what I might do to him. He'd fought too fearlessly earlier to care about what became of himself. Rather he wisely realized Olivia and her sister had no other choice. They were my prisoners and there was nothing he or anyone else could do about it.

Finally, she straightened her shoulders and held her head high. Contempt flashed in her eyes. "Very well, sir. I will surrender to you as long as you vow you will leave my household unharmed."

"You have my word." I had a sudden urge to correct the way she'd addressed me. As the oldest son, I'd inherited my father's title, Baron of Windsor. The proper address was *my lord* or Lord Windsor. *Sir* was the address given to untitled knights, not lords of manors.

Somehow, I sensed that such titles were very important to Lady Olivia, that she might respect me more if I revealed my true identity. Yet, in the year I'd been working for Pitt, I'd neglected my titles and privileges. By doing so, I'd hoped to forget my old life and all the pain that had accompanied it.

I'd worked hard and kept myself busy enough that the pain had turned into a dull ache locked away in the deep parts of my mind. And that's where I wanted it to stay. It was better that way. For everybody.

If Lady Olivia wanted to believe she was superior to me, I had no need to prove otherwise. She was simply my prisoner. My job was to deliver her to Pitt. Once I accomplished that, I'd never have to speak with her again.

Chapter 3

I scanned the barren heathland. There were so few hiding places. When I escaped with Izzy— and I would escape—I needed more cover besides the heather and gorse and the occasional orchids with their white flowering spikes poking above the other vegetation like white flags of surrender.

Had I done the right thing in surrendering to Lord Pitt's commander?

Izzy rode sidesaddle on her gentle mare next to my sturdy bay. In the heat of the June day, she'd gradually wilted as the day had progressed, like a primrose without a proper watering. Her light veil had provided some protection from the unrelenting sun, but the hard riding and the heat had taken their toll upon her. Her head bobbed as she dozed, and I woke her only when she was in danger of sliding off.

Truthfully, the heat had sapped me of much needed energy as well. Now with onset of twilight, I prayed we'd both have the necessary fortitude to sneak away.

We needed to do so before we were out of the Marches and too far away to seek aid. Of course we couldn't return to Ludlow. Though Sir Aldric had burned only a few buildings and left most of the structure intact, we would find no refuge there, not with the walls down and the supplies ransacked.

Rather, we would ride north to Depnor Castle and find sanctuary with the Marquess of Clearwater and Lionel. It was a full day's hard ride, but we could do most of it under the cover of darkness—at least I hoped so. Even though our mounts would be tired, we would gain a lead and stay well ahead of any party that might come after us.

Ahead, Sir Aldric rode a powerful warhorse and led his band of knights, forcing Izzy and me to ride at the center of the party, with the supply wagons bringing up the rear.

The commander hadn't spoken to me again since he'd left my chambers. He'd been too busy overseeing the pillage within the keep to stand guard over Izzy and me and had instead given us into the care of his knights while we'd dressed for traveling and packed a few clothing items.

They'd behaved honorably toward us for which I was grateful.

Now those knights rode in a tight formation around us, always vigilant, hemming us in so that we could go nowhere but forward.

Perhaps Sir Aldric feared my father might be on his trail. I could only pray he was, that he'd arrived at Ludlow Castle today, found Cecil bound tightly to the chair, and learned of our fate.

Whatever the case, I was confident Father would send a regiment to rescue Izzy and me just as soon as he heard of our capture. While he'd never been kind and warm like Mother, he was loyal, always loyal.

"You must put aside your own desires for those of your family, Olivia," he'd said to me often when I was growing up. "Your personal wishes must remain secondary to family. Family comes first above all else."

It was my duty to do whatever I could to help my father as he worked to maintain power and prestige among his peers. Then he'd be able to make a prized match for Izzy, just as he was doing for me. And he'd be able to pay for the rare medicines that would possibly cure Charles of his ailments.

Yes, Father would send a search party to rescue us. But if he didn't immediately get word of our capture, he'd be delayed in coming after us. In the meantime, I'd need to do all I could to escape from Lord Pitt's clutches. Surely, at some point, I'd find a weakness among Sir Aldric's men and their ability to keep watch, and when I did, I'd take full advantage of it.

What I hadn't yet figured out was why Lord Pitt wanted Izzy and me. From the moment his army had surrounded Ludlow, I'd suspected this had something to do with an offense my father had committed. He was a powerful man in the kingdom and had developed many enemies. There were even some who accused him of having secret alliances with the Welsh. Of course, all the baron magnates who lived in the Marcher borderlands came under suspicion of forming bonds with the neighboring Welsh, especially those like Father who were critical of the king from time to time.

Even so, I couldn't decide what charges Lord Pitt planned to level against my father and why he'd taken Izzy and me as his prisoners. If I'd had time to speak further with Sir Aldric, I would have interrogated him for the information.

My sights strayed to his rigid back, his broad shoulders, and the mail hood that now replaced the plate armor. Without his helmet, I'd briefly glimpsed his profile and had been surprised to see how young he was. I'd expected someone much older and seasoned from years of battle, not a handsome warrior.

Somehow knowing he was young and tough made the loss of my battle with him earlier sting a little less. If he'd been older with slower reflexes, perhaps I could have overpowered him. Whatever the case, I took satisfaction in the fact that I'd surprised him with my identity. I'd fought well enough under the circumstances that he hadn't realized I was a woman until Izzy had made mention of it.

Shouts drew my attention forward, and I soon discovered we were making camp for the night. A narrow gorge ahead contained a creek, which would provide refreshment not only for us but for our horses. As we came upon the gorge, I was pleased to see that tall grass and tangled brush bordered it. While not woodland or rock outcroppings, the brush would give Izzy and me some shelter during our getaway.

All the while we ate our simple dinner of roasted lamb and barley bread, I used the remaining daylight to plot our escape route. When darkness finally fell, and we retired for the night, I was grateful for the small tent one of the knights erected for us.

I wasn't sure what treatment prisoners usually received, but I suspected most weren't given the deference of a warm meal, much less a tent of their own. Sir Aldric had indicated that Lord Pitt wanted us alive, possibly unharmed.

But that didn't mean the captain was required to be polite and kind. I'd heard enough stories over the years to know that captured women and children were often considered dispensable—nothing more than spoils of war to be used up and cast aside.

Yet the knights under Sir Aldric's command hadn't so much as looked at us, had in fact treated us with the utmost courtesy.

I unrolled the blanket the guard had given us and spread it over the dry grass. Izzy brushed her hair in silence, likely mulling over my whispered instructions regarding our escape plans.

"Lady Olivia," came Sir Aldric's voice from outside the tent.

I stood as best I could under the low canopy ceiling. "You may enter," I replied as I smoothed my skirt, wrinkled and dusty from the day.

The tent flap opened and the captain ducked inside. The fire pit outside our tent provided the only light, but it was enough for me to see that he'd discarded his mail hood. His hair was overlong and pulled back into a leather strap. It was dark in color to match the shadows on his jaw and cheeks, the unshaven scruff, the remnants of the past week of living on the battlefield.

When he straightened, I was caught off guard at how handsome he was in a rugged, almost dangerous way. His features were strong like granite, his jaw and chin chiseled, his nose perfectly balanced. Most remarkable were his eyes—deep blue, unfathomable, and haunted.

Even in the faint light, those eyes drew me in, beckoning me to soothe whatever hurts he'd experienced.

"How do you fare?" he asked. "Have you need of anything?"

His questions should have surprised me. But after the civility he'd already shown, his continued kindness was strangely calming. I was having a difficult time holding on to my disdain for him. I quickly reminded myself he'd commanded the troops that had surrounded and invaded my home. He'd wreaked destruction against my people, servants, and knights. He'd fought against Cecil and me in my chambers and would have killed us if not for discovering I was a woman. He was forcibly taking me away as a prisoner.

He was the enemy.

"We are faring as well as can be under the circumstances." I tried to stay hardened and aloof.

He glanced around the tent, taking in every detail from our small chest to the silver brush that lay idle in Izzy's hands to the blanket I'd spread. Even in the dim lighting, he didn't seem to miss a detail. As his attention shifted back to our chest, I held my breath.

I could sense his desire to search our belongings again. His knights had already done so once before loading our chest into the back of a wagon. His keenness to check again showed him for the wise and capable commander he was.

And yet, he retreated a step out the open tent flap, too respectful and noble to rummage through our clothing and personal items. Little did he know that his kindness would be his downfall.

"I'll send a guard to awaken you before first light," he said, bowing his head. "We will depart at break of dawn."

"Very well." I kept my tone cool, hoping my detached mask was firmly in place. If this man caught a whiff of any anxiety or duplicity, he'd surely be on high alert. But if he believed I was angry with him for my captivity, then he'd leave me alone with no thought to my plotting.

With a final glance at me, he ducked out and let the flap fall into place.

When he was gone, I expelled a long breath.

Once Izzy and I finally lay down, she curled against me. Although the heat of the day had dissipated with the set of darkness, I knew Izzy wasn't seeking warmth from me. Rather she needed my comfort.

With her smaller, more delicate hand in

mine, I squeezed. "We shall be fine, Izzy. Now sleep for a little while."

She expelled a trusting breath and was quiet for so long a moment I almost believed she'd fallen asleep.

"What does Lord Pitt intend to do to us?" Her whisper was wobbly and followed by a sniffle.

"Nothing," I replied. "We shall never see him."

"But what if we cannot get away?"

"We shall."

"Does he intend to make us his servants? Or perhaps force us to marry his knights? Or maybe sell us to foreign rulers?"

"No." I closed my mind against such possibilities, although none of them were without merit. Lord Pitt had gained a reputation for having a strong alliance with the king. If my father had done something to displease the king, there was no telling what Lord Pitt might do with us.

All the more reason to make our getaway once the camp was quiet and settled for the night.

"Lord Pitt likely has a grievance against Father," I whispered. "He will retain us only until Father makes amends."

Holding prisoners of war for ransom was a common practice, especially among the nobility.

Again, the tales of woe from such practices were far more plentiful than the tales that ended well. Usually the noblemen held for ransom sat in dungeons for months while families scrambled to come up with enough to free them. Sometimes the noblemen were killed out of impatience. Other times, they died from cold and starvation.

"I cannot keep my fear at bay," Izzy whispered.

I bent toward my sister and kissed her head. "I shall ensure your safety, Izzy. Now go to sleep."

My reassurance was apparently enough. Within minutes, her breathing evened, and her body sagged in the weariness of slumber. I allowed myself to doze for a little while too, knowing I'd need all my energy for later.

When I awoke, I wasn't sure how much time had passed, but the silence in the camp indicated now was the time to make our escape. I arose stealthily and dug through the chest until my fingers connected with the false bottom. With the click of the hidden lever, I located the knife Cecil had hidden there a day ago when he'd advised me to use the chest in the case of an evacuation or capture.

I pried the knife loose and carefully slit the canvas at the rear of the tent. From what I'd ascertained, Sir Aldric had only posted one guard at the front opening. He assumed two unarmed noblewomen would be helpless, that he had no need of extra precautions the way he might for a man.

In fact, I doubted he would have given a man the privacy of a tent, likely would have chained him, and kept him under careful watch.

A twinge of guilt pricked me. I was breaking the commander's trust and spurning his chivalry to me as a woman. Just as quickly as the prick came, I smoothed it away with assertion that he was getting only what he deserved for taking us against our will. Lord Pitt could have worked out his grievances with my father in some other manner that didn't involve our abduction.

When I sliced an opening large enough to squeeze through, I woke Izzy and cautioned her against any sound. Using the stealth and silence Cecil had taught me, I crawled out motioning Izzy to follow my every move as carefully and quietly as possible.

We crept along the ground in the darkness, following the route I'd mentally planned, dodging the other guards who kept watch over the camp. The knights were alert to any movement and noises outside the camp but wouldn't be paying attention to rustle from within—or at least that's what I was counting on.

We slithered among the gorse and heather,

and it seemed to take hours to reach the creek bed. Once we were there, we skirted the horses so that we wouldn't cause any of them to shift or snort or make any other noises that might draw notice from the guards.

"Stay here," I whispered to Izzy from a low spot near the water's edge behind a tangled clump of gorse. "I shall be back in a few minutes."

"Where are you going?" Her whisper was threaded with anxiety.

"I need to cut my horse loose." I'd already decided we could only chance freeing one of our horses. Mine was the better of the two choices. He was sturdier and could carry both of us for a longer distance. I'd also used him in my training over the past few years. I was counting on him slowly working his way out of the herd and then following my trail to where I'd be waiting for him upstream.

Crouched low, I crept past the horses, doing my best to stay close to the ground so they wouldn't catch my scent. Several of their ears pricked as I approached, but I was silent enough that they didn't bother with me.

When I reached my horse, I let my fingers glide along his flank, assuring him of my presence. At his soft nickering welcome, I held myself motionless, praying none of the guards would observe me among the dark shadows.

Finally, I lifted my knife and sawed through the lead rope that bound the horse to the others. As the fastening fell, I brushed my hand over his muzzle and nostrils, letting him breathe me in.

I backed away, this time wading in the creek, heedless of the cold water seeping into my boots. I'd take off my shoes later and let them dry tomorrow. But for now, I had to use the soft trickle of the creek to mask my steps.

I reached the gorse bush and Izzy well ahead of the horse. As we waited, my heart thudded with the need to be on our way. We'd taken longer than I'd anticipated, and our lead was diminishing with every passing second.

I'd almost given up hope my horse would reach us, when his soft nicker greeted us. "Let us make haste," I whispered to Izzy as I reached for her hand. "Stay low until we are well out of sight."

For several minutes, we crept down the creek bank using only the light of the stars to guide our way, until at last I could no longer see any traces of camp. I halted and allowed myself a moment of exaltation. Although we still had a long ride ahead of us, I knew Cecil would be proud of me for escaping undetected.

"We are far enough away to ride." I released Izzy's hand and patted my horse. "I shall help you mount."

She didn't respond. Instead she stiffened and

sucked in a sharp breath.

"Ready?" I cupped my hands to form a step for her. I didn't like the idea of riding bareback any more than she did. But we had no choice. Retrieving the saddle would have cost us time we didn't have.

"Come now, Izzy."

"And where, pray tell, are you ladies going?" At the question spoken in a low voice, my heart plummeted with dread.

I pivoted to find Sir Aldric watching me. Under the faint starlight, his features were an unyielding marble grooved with slanted angry lines. Next to him, another knight had captured Izzy and held her with both arms twisted behind her back.

Without giving the two a moment to prepare for an attack, I lunged with my knife and stabbed it into the knight holding Izzy.

He cried out and recoiled, letting go of my sister and falling away from the knife. I grabbed Izzy, threw her behind me, and ducked to escape Sir Aldric as he reached for me.

"Get on the horse, Izzy," I shouted at her, even as I dodged another of Sir Aldric's snaking arms. Behind me, Izzy had stumbled to the ground and was scrambling to regain her footing. I had to hold off Sir Aldric a few more seconds while she mounted. Even if I couldn't escape with her, I could at least send her away and pray she would find the way to Lionel and Depnor Castle without me.

As Sir Aldric lunged for me again, I swept the knife at him. He jolted back before it could slit his throat, but the tip grazed his cheek, drawing a thin line.

He lifted his fingers to his face and tested the slickness of his blood, as if he couldn't believe a noblewoman had dared to harm him.

"Make haste, Izzy." I lifted the knife and took another swipe at Sir Aldric. Out of the corner of my eye, I could see that the other knight was straightening and recovering from the initial shock and pain of his wound.

At the rasp of his sword against his sheath, I didn't have to see to know he was advancing upon me.

"No," Sir Aldric barked. "Put your weapon away. I shall deal with the girl."

Girl? Did he think I was as helpless and incapable as a child?

"Get the horse," Sir Aldric ordered his companion even as he circled me, eyeing my knife, the blade dark with blood.

I kept pace with his movements, attempting to gauge his next move so I could be prepared. My muscles tensed and I tightened my grip on the knife.

Behind me, my horse whinnied and protested the other knight's approach. In that moment, I realized Izzy wouldn't be able to mount without my help. If I told her to run, where would she go? She wouldn't make it far on her own.

The frustration of my foiled plans emboldened me. Without warning, I broke forward and jumped at Sir Aldric. Though I moved swiftly and brought my knife down forcefully, this time he caught my arm and jerked it up. The sharpness wrenched my socket and seemed to tear my arm from my body.

Even though I didn't want to scream, I did. The pain in my joint was excruciating. His thumbs pressed into my wrist forcing my grip off the knife so that it clattered to the ground. In an instant, he twisted both of my arms behind my back so that I couldn't breathe through the pain. I sucked in a gasping breath and blinked to keep myself from passing out.

"Now, where did you say you were going, my lady?" he growled.

I bit back my angry retort. He may have stopped me this time. But I'd find a way to escape. Eventually.

Chapter 4

LADY OLIVIA WOULD BE THE DEATH OF ME.

At the scuffle from behind, I didn't have to swivel in my saddle to know she was causing trouble. Again.

I glanced at the position of the sun in the sky and reined my mount. I had to laud her for her determination. In addition to her plot of the previous night, she'd managed four other slips this day—two times while supposedly relieving herself, once at the noon meal, and then another when we'd dismounted to ford a stream.

The delays had cost me hours of crucial travel time. Our progress was already encumbered by the wagonloads of goods we were hauling away from Ludlow Castle. With each of Lady Olivia's escapades, we lagged even further behind schedule.

I had no doubt that as soon as word reached

the Earl of Ulster regarding the ransacking of his estate along with the seizure of his daughters, he'd send a well-armed war party after us. I suspected now Lady Olivia was purposefully making excuses to stop, so her rescuers would have time to catch up to us. Although our efforts against Ludlow hadn't been taxing and my men were still relatively strong and fit for battle, we were in no position to defend ourselves, especially out in the open heathland.

I'd hoped to reach the wooded area on the western borders of Pitt's land where we would be within a day's ride of Bevins of Lowdown, in familiar territory as well as close to reinforcements. But with dusk only a couple hours' ride away, and at the rate we were going, we'd be lucky to make it to the next watering hole.

As our entourage came to a halt, I backtracked to the center of our party where Lady Olivia and Lady Isabelle were surrounded by my strongest and most trusted warriors.

The summer sun was still hot upon my chain mail, sweltering me under the layers. My mouth was parched. And I had little patience for the pampered noblewomen in my care. But I made myself approach calmly.

Lady Olivia's sharp commands to one of the knights punctuated the dry air. She'd dismounted and was in the process of helping her sister down from her horse. Darien stood next to her and was attempting to stop her without touching her. I'd warned my men not to lay a hand on the women unless I explicitly gave them permission as I had last night with Perceval when he'd captured Lady Isabelle.

Of course, I hadn't expected Lady Olivia to stab Perceval or to lash out at me. Even if her efforts had been weak and the wounds superficial, I'd realized in that moment I'd severely underestimated her. I touched my cheek where her cut still stung.

"You cannot expect us to continue on endlessly without giving us the opportunity to relieve ourselves." Olivia reached for Isabelle's hand and beckoned her down.

"But my lady." Darien spoke forcefully as he attempted to tug Isabelle's horse away from Olivia. "We stopped less than an hour ago—"

"Nature has no regard for the passing of time." She sidestepped him.

Darien caught sight of me, and the relief that came over his countenance would have been comical if I were in a laughing mood.

I'd attempted to treat her as any lady deserved. But at every turn she abused the privileges and courtesy I bestowed upon her. Even now, her expression told me she'd figured out she had an advantage over my knights, that they were too polite to lay a hand on her to stop her whims.

I nudged my horse closer, my ire flaring into

flame as it had last night after she'd slashed my face. I hadn't meant to cause her so much pain when I'd disarmed her, and I'd rebuked myself sternly the rest of the night for it. I'd decided I would apologize and had almost worked up the nerve, until she'd attempted another escape and my remorse had fled as quickly as the dawn.

"My lady," I said. "Since you are experiencing so much discomfort with your mount and are needing to stop so frequently, I have devised a new strategy to ensure swifter traveling."

She didn't spare me a glance over her shoulder as she began to help Isabelle from her mare. The younger girl slid down into Olivia's waiting arms, clearly weary and having no energy to resist Olivia's ploys, although I suspected she was accustomed to her older sister's scheming.

I hopped down from my mount, aware the attention was squarely upon me, that I would set the tone for my men in their treatment of our prisoners. As much as I wanted to toss Lady Olivia back upon her steed, if I resorted to rudeness and manhandling, my men would soon follow suit.

As Olivia slipped an arm around Isabelle's waist, the red-haired beauty cast accusing eyes upon me, rebuking me for Isabelle's weariness. I wanted to remind Olivia she was to blame for Isabelle's lack of sleep last night. If she'd slumbered instead of so foolishly trying to escape, then Isabelle wouldn't be as tired.

Instead of reminding her, I forced myself to react with the cool detachment that would show her I was in command and that she didn't have the power to anger me, even though she had. "As Lady Isabelle is taxed beyond endurance, she will ride with Sir Darien."

I nodded at Darien. His eyes widened in surprise. But when I glanced pointedly at Lady Isabelle and then at his horse, he jumped into action to obey my directive.

"No," Olivia protested as Darien reached for Lady Isabelle. "She will share my mount."

"That won't be possible, my lady." I closed the gap between myself and Olivia. "Since you will be riding with me." Before she could figure out her next move, I encircled her waist with my hands. In one rapid move, I lifted her upward onto my waiting horse, giving her no choice but to grab onto the pommel.

Immediately I swung up behind her.

In spite of her long skirt and chemise tangling in her legs, she did her best to scramble down the other side of the horse away from me. But I wound my arm around her middle and held her firmly in the saddle, which wasn't roomy enough to hold both of us without squeezing us tightly together.

"I insist that you put me down at once," she said even as she struggled to twist out of my grip.

Conscious of our audience, I maintained my composure. "My lady, since your own horse has given you such trouble and has wearied you, I am certain you will find this new arrangement more to your liking."

"You are entirely wrong, sir." She attempted to pry my gloved hand loose from her hip.

I clicked my tongue and my horse lurched forward, forcing Olivia into my chest. I used the opportunity to pin her even tighter, giving her no room at all to wiggle away.

She stiffened and gave an unladylike huff. But I only urged my mount to a trot. I could sense she had too much pride to thrash and claw at my hold, though her rigid posture told me she clearly wanted to fight her way free.

As I resumed my place at the front of my men, her fingers wrapped around mine, attempting to pry my hold loose. She dug her nails into my arm where my mail and gloves met.

Of course, I didn't budge. She could endeavor to free herself and hurt me all she wanted, but I wouldn't relent. She'd learn it soon enough.

After some time, she stilled. Although she didn't speak, her loathing was evident in every hard muscle. We rode in silence, which was fine with me. I had no desire to spar words. My job was simply to deliver her to Pitt unharmed, and I'd do it even if I had to make her ride on my horse with me the rest of the way.

As the hour passed, her body gradually relaxed. Although I didn't let my guard down, it was clear she was tired and couldn't stay angry forever. When she finally allowed her head to rest against my chest, I chanced a glance down to see her long lashes fall to her pale cheeks. She was struggling to stay awake.

Perhaps sensing my glance, her eyes flew open. She cast me a sideways look. I stared straight ahead and pretended I hadn't noticed her. Next time I looked, her eyes were closed again. And this time they didn't open.

While she slept, I gave in to the temptation to study her profile, noting as I had when I'd yanked off her helmet just how beautiful she was. Her features were elegant, her skin like fine rare pearls, and her red hair thick and lustrous.

In slumber, her perpetual glare and scowl had softened, and I felt almost sorry for her. She hadn't asked for all this—being captured, forced to leave her home, and made to ride long hours in the summer heat. Even though I was frustrated by all the trouble she'd caused me during our journey, I couldn't blame her for trying to free herself and her sister whose freedom she clearly cared about more than her own.

She was only doing what I would have if our roles had been reversed.

Nevertheless, I must fulfill my duty to Pitt and the king. They needed to bring the Earl of Ulster into submission, and apparently holding his daughters ransom was the way they planned to do it.

When twilight began to fall, I pushed the troops onward, even though my stomach ached with the pangs of hunger. I sensed when Olivia awoke by the sudden stiffening in her body, as though she'd forgotten where she was while she slept and had just remembered.

For a time, she attempted to hold herself aloof. But eventually, as earlier, she succumbed to the ease of leaning against my chest and resting in my hold. Although I'd loosened my grip, I kept one arm firmly locked around her middle while guiding the horse with my other. And while we were squeezed tightly into the saddle, I didn't feel cramped, especially when she melded into me and simply rode with the motion of the horse.

We traveled late, until we finally reached a wellspring where our horses could be replenished. We hadn't gone as far as I'd originally planned, but I'd pushed as hard as I could for the day.

When I assisted Olivia from the horse, she swayed, unsteady on her feet. I rapidly reached for her, my hands going to her waist.

However, the moment I touched her, she recoiled as if I'd bitten her, as if the past several hours of our close proximity had never occurred, as if I hadn't just been holding her against my chest with my arms wrapped around her.

She started to stagger away from me. But I'd learned enough about her to realize she would try to escape again the first chance she had, and that the only way to stop her from running away was to keep her at my side.

I snagged her arm before she could go far.

"What?" she asked, all traces of slumber gone from her face, replaced with sharp alertness. "Will you prevent me a moment of privacy even now?"

I knew I needed to command one of my men to take over guarding her. Other matters needed my attention, and someone else could play nursemaid to this young woman. Nevertheless, the thought of handing her over to my men sent a strange patter of trepidation through me.

She'd proven to be too difficult for them. If I released her, she'd only cause more trouble, perhaps burn down the camp or take someone hostage or worse. My thoughts returned to the knife she'd plunged into Perceval last night. Even if the wound wasn't deep or serious, and he was none the worse for it, I had no doubt she'd do it again if she got her hands on a weapon of any kind.

"You surely do not intend to chain me to your person." Her voice was laced with irritation.

"As a matter of fact, that's exactly what I was planning." I hadn't considered it, but something in her tone stoked my own ire. Perhaps the greatest way to annoy her in return was to make her do the thing she loathed the most—spend time with me.

"Since you are quite determined to make trouble for me any way you can conceive, you've given me no choice but to keep you by my side at all times."

Around us, with torches now lit, my men had begun setting up camp, attending to the various duties I'd assigned to them at the outset of the campaign. Some would see to the horses, others would stand guard, and still others would oversee and assist the servants in preparing the evening meal.

Sir Darien approached with Lady Isabelle. He led her carefully as though she might break at any moment. Although Isabelle was wrinkled and dusty with travel, she smiled sweetly at Darien and complied with his directives. She behaved as a noblewoman should—docilely, kindly, and gratefully.

Unlike Olivia.

I leveled a censuring glare at the strong-willed woman, hoping she could read my admonition to act more like her younger sister.

"There you are, my lady," Darien said stopping in front of Olivia. At Olivia's slicing glare, he released Isabelle's arm and stepped away from her.

"I thank you, sir," Isabelle said demurely. "You have been most kind."

Darien bowed his head, the silver links of his mail hood glistening against the torchlight. Even as he lowered his head, he couldn't hide his admiration for the young noblewoman. While Isabelle lacked Olivia's sharp, stunning beauty, she was still pretty in a soft, luminous way.

Seeing Darien's infatuation, Olivia's scowl deepened. He was a good-looking young man, and at eighteen years he was the youngest in the group, having recently been knighted for his brave deeds. He'd lived with Pitt for many years as a page and squire long before my arrival. He was from a wealthy family in the north, a second son, without inheritance, who would someday need to make his own fortune.

For now, however, I could give him a small measure of enjoyment and at the same time irk Olivia further.

"Sir Darien, you will guard Lady Isabelle the rest of the trip," I said without swerving my attention from Olivia's face.

She sucked in a breath and swung icy eyes upon me. "She has no need of a guard."

"Perhaps not quite as much as you, my lady." I held in a satisfied smile. "But Sir Darien will keep your sister company since she'll no longer have the pleasure of being with you."

Darien's head had snapped up, and he looked between Olivia and me, confusion in his guileless eyes.

"I shall not allow it." Olivia jerked her arm, trying to break free of my grasp, but I didn't relent.

"Sir Darien, before you assist Lady Isabelle to her tent, you must do one thing."

"Yes, Captain?" He cast a sideways glance at Isabelle, his face alight with the excitement of his new duty.

"Find a chain and bind Lady Olivia to me."

Chapter
5

I couldn't roll without the chain clinking.
Therefore, I lay on my back on the bedroll Sir
Aldric had placed next to his. The ground was
too hard and lumpy, and I hadn't been able to
get comfortable since lying down.

The camp was silent except for the crackle
of the fire and the raspy croaking of toads near
the watering hole. The darkness of the sky
overhead was broken only by thin wispy clouds
that shrouded the moon, parting now and then
to allow a glow to fall over the camp.

Sir Aldric's breathing was heavy and even—
the sign that he'd succumbed to his exhaustion.

I peered again at him sideways, to the place
where my chain bound me to him. The clamp
was locked securely around his bicep as surely
as mine was locked around my wrist. I'd already
attempted slipping the clamp off over my hand.

But it was on tight—not enough to chaff my skin, but certainly not comfortable.

I had no idea where the key was. Even if I'd known, I wouldn't be able to get to it, not without knocking Sir Aldric out and dragging him with me. But he'd left me no opportunity to do so, clearing away anything I might use as a weapon, even sticks and rocks. After my attempt at picking the lock, he'd even confiscated my hairpins, so that I was forced to braid my hair and use a leather strap to confine it.

Sir Aldric had finally wised up and stopped trusting me. Even so, he'd still done his best to offer me every courtesy a lady deserved. I had to give him credit for that. Although he was making me sleep outside tonight, rather than in the tent with Isabelle, he'd provided a spot away from his men and yet close to the fire.

I let my sights travel from his bicep to his broad shoulder to his neck and then to his jaw and chin and nose. Although the nick I'd given him last night wasn't deep, guilt twisted at my stomach for having lashed out at him. I should have known I'd be no match against so strong a man. Even in sleep, he held himself rigid, his strength evident in every tense muscle. Fully clothed and still in chain mail, he had only a blanket tucked under his head for comfort.

As before, I was struck by his strong,

handsome features as well as how young he was for a captain. How had he gained such a position? Where was he from? And had he left a wife behind somewhere? He was surely of an age where his parents had formed an advantageous match for him.

"You must like what you see, my lady," came his low whisper.

The comment startled me, and my attention darted to the gauzy clouds in front of the moon. If I'd been a blushing woman, my cheeks would have been red. But thankfully, I'd mastered the ability to remain composed. "I was only plotting how I might slit your throat."

He rolled on to his back and crossed his arms over his chest, clanking the chain and pulling it taut. "You may admit your attraction. I won't hold it against you."

My annoyance flared as quickly as a flame fanned by bellows—more annoyance at myself than him for being caught staring. "You think too highly of yourself."

"I wasn't the one staring for the past hour."

"I have not stared for an hour." I hadn't stared for such lengths, had I? But even as I voiced my denial, I knew I was guilty of letting my sights drift to his face too often.

His response was a slight curve in his lips, the beginning of a grin. The first I'd seen from him. I was chagrinned to realize the upturn only added to his charm and made me want to stare at him again.

I silently berated myself. "You surely have a wife or betrothed to feed your inflated pride and have no need of further flattery."

As quickly as his smile came, it vanished. In its place was the haunted sadness I'd noticed the first time I'd seen his face.

"My wife is dead." His low tone told me more than any words could—that he'd loved deeply and hadn't recovered from his loss.

From the tight clamp of his lips and the twitch in his jaw, I sensed this was the end of our conversation—if it could even be called a conversation. Up to this point, we hadn't spoken to each other more than absolutely necessary, or at least that had been my policy during the few times he'd attempted to talk.

But for a reason I couldn't explain, I felt as though I should say something more, that I couldn't let the issue rest without showing a measure of compassion. He wouldn't need my condolences or sympathy. As a strong man, he would only loathe such coddling. Instead, he would appreciate the same as I would—bluntness.

"The strongest of us feel pain the deepest."

He stared unseeingly at the dark night sky.

"I cannot fathom what you went through, but I know I would not want to live if anything happened to my sister."

He was silent for so long I began to consider that we would speak no more for the night.

"I did try to kill myself," he finally whispered. "But self-destruction only makes the pain worse, especially for the other people you love."

His words rang with wisdom borne of sorrow and pain. And I could not stop a seedling of admiration from sprouting.

"What kind of self-destruction?" I forged ahead with my blunt question. I wouldn't ask him about his wife. That was hallowed ground, and no one deserved to tread there unless invited. But now that he was talking about his regrets, I was curious to know more about this noble captor of mine.

"I drank and gambled until I was in debt to nearly every lord in the southern part of the realm, including Lord Pitt. He gave me the chance to pay off my debts, but I squandered the opportunity. He had no alternative but to attack. The siege cost many lives and almost destroyed my family and home." Sir Aldric grew quiet as if the memory of the past was too much to bear.

I tried to make sense of everything he'd revealed. "So you are also a prisoner of Lord Pitt? He took you captive when he attacked your home?"

"No. I handed myself over to him and bound myself to his service so I could protect my family as well as repay the debt I owed him twice over."

I pushed myself up onto one elbow and openly studied this man, seeing him with new eyes. I didn't know of any nobleman who would subject himself to the humiliation of becoming the bondservant of another nobleman.

"So this," I motioned to the nearby wagons loaded with the goods he'd taken from my home. "This is how you repay your debt to Lord Pitt?"

"I have already repaid it." He still stared straight up at the darkness overhead, the muscles in his jaw flexing.

"Then you are free to return to your home?"

"There is no reason for me to return home."

I was tempted to ask him what had become of his family. But as with probing about his wife, I decided not to go where I had not been invited. Instead I said the only other thing that came to mind. "Do you believe you will only have one chance at love? Or will you make room in your heart eventually for another?"

"I will never make room for anyone else," he said low and hard. "I don't deserve another chance." His guilt and sadness grooved lines in his forehead and at the corners of his eyes, lines I suddenly wished I could smooth out. Surely no matter his past mistakes, he could make amends and one day live a full and satisfying life again.

Before I could formulate a response, he shifted and I found myself the object of his penetrating gaze. "What about you, my lady? You speak of love. Will you have a love match with Lord Clearwater?"

His mention of Lionel startled me. "How do you know of the possibility of my union with Lord Clearwater?"

"Surely you don't think I would set out on this mission for Lord Pitt without being fully informed regarding every detail of your father and his family."

"Why should Lord Pitt take interest in my betrothal to Lord Clearwater?"

"Are you betrothed?" Again his gaze probed deeply.

"Not yet," I admitted. "But it is imminent."

"Lionel is a scoundrel like his father."

I bristled at the accusation. "You have no reason to speak ill of people when you are not acquainted with them."

"I know them well enough."

"Clearly you do not—"

"The marquess and other Marcher barons have been seeking an alliance with the Welsh so they can rise up against the king."

Sir Aldric's pronouncement silenced the protest on the tip of my tongue. Instead, I watched his face, searching for evidence of truth, but knowing from the heavy weight upon my heart he was not lying. He was giving voice to rumors I'd already heard.

"You believe my father is working with the Marquess of Clearwater to lead a rebellion against the king?"

"I would not hold you or your sister against your will if I didn't believe it was true."

From everything I'd learned so far about Sir Aldric, I believed he was a man of honor—one who wouldn't approve of taking noblewomen into captivity unless for a greater purpose.

Now I understood what that greater purpose was. "By capturing Izzy and me, does Lord Pitt hope to bring my father into an alliance with him instead of the marquess?"

"Lord Pitt is seeking only to protect the king."

My stomach churned with the implications of everything Sir Aldric had revealed. "What will Lord Pitt require of my father to gain our freedom?"

"A ransom, of course."

"And . . ."

"And that he pledge his loyalty to the king."

"If he does not?"

"Lord Pitt will attack him again."

A cold dread seized me at the prospect of Lord Pitt inflicting any more pain upon my family. What else could he do except . . .

"Next time he will go after your brother, Charles." Sir Aldric spoke gravely, as if he'd heard my thoughts.

I shook my head. "But he's sick—"

"Which is why Lord Pitt showed mercy on your father by taking you and your sister."

I collapsed against my bedroll. I couldn't stop icy fingers from creeping around my heart. I'd been so sure Father would ride after us and attempt to regain our freedom, that he'd pay the ransom, that he'd do whatever he could to protect me and Izzy.

But if he was forming an alliance with other Marcher barons to rise up against the king, would he rescue us or would he sacrifice us as part of the cost of war?

I shook my head. Father was loyal to his family. He'd do whatever it took to gain our release. He'd not only do it because he loved us but because he wanted to keep Charles from becoming the next target. In Charles's weakened condition, captivity would kill him.

Surely Father wasn't so opposed to the king that he would refuse to turn from plotting rebellion.

Even as I sought to defend my father, I couldn't scatter my suspicions. Words Father had spoken over the years whispered at the back of my mind—his displeasure over the way the king treated the Marcher barons, for calling upon them last when in need of defenses, for allowing so few of them to court, for accusing them of having mixed blood from intermarrying too often with the Welsh.

What would happen to Izzy and me if Father decided not to comply with Lord Pitt's demands?

I closed my eyes, not wanting to think about the possibility. I could sense Sir Aldric watching me, but I turned my face away from him. If he hoped to sway me against my father, he was mistaken. He was my family. I would do whatever I had to for him, even if I had to sacrifice myself in the process.

Chapter 6

I was keenly aware of Sir Aldric's hand upon my waist, much more this new day than I had been the previous eve. I was also keenly aware of his broad chest against my back.

When he'd lifted me into his saddle at break of dawn, I'd protested. But as he slid up behind me and encircled me, I found my breath and my protest cut off by his nearness. I told myself my easy acquiescence had more to do with his nighttime revelations and my growing sympathy for him than with his handsome presence.

Before leaving camp, he'd taken off the chain that had bound us. But I knew from yesterday, I wouldn't have any chance of escaping, at least not while hemmed in by Sir Aldric atop his horse.

With each passing hour, I grew more attuned

to his movements, to the places his body pressed against mine, and to the steady rise and fall of his breathing.

The day was gray with the dampness of rain hanging in the air. The slightly cooler temperatures made the ride less tiresome. Even though I was sore from traveling, I found myself in better spirits than yesterday.

Izzy rode her own horse not far behind me with the young knight, Sir Darien, constantly by her side. Though at first I'd been irritated that Sir Aldric had made the arrangement for the knight to attend Izzy, I saw the wisdom in it now. He acted as a personal bodyguard more than a jailor, and I could rest assured she was safe. Sir Darien's flattery and adoration were harmless. And Izzy was as innocent and unaware, as usual, of the effect she had on men.

While I never stopped plotting how I might save her from this captivity, I found myself relaxing in the knowledge that Sir Aldric and his men meant us no harm—at least for now.

Throughout the morning, we talked of mostly inconsequential things—like our experiences with hunting and hawking. Although Sir Aldric never boasted, I could tell he was every bit as skilled a hunter as he was commander.

"Ahead is Bevins of Lowdown," he said. "An excellent boar hunting ground."

On the horizon loomed a heavily wooded

forest with dogwoods all along the edge. The sight of the forest confirmed what I'd suspected—that we were nearing Lord Pitt's land. Once we crossed over, I would lose any remaining chance of escape.

"You need to plan a boar hunt soon, Sir Aldric," I said. "And since I have never gone, you must allow me to accompany you."

He leaned in slightly and his breath brushed my temple. "If I plan a hunt, how do I know you'll not run away the first chance you have?" His voice rumbled softly so that my belly turned over in a strange flip.

"You may chain me to your personage again."

"I fear I may need to chain you close at all times regardless of where we are or what we are doing."

"Would that be so terrible, sir?" I tried to keep my voice light.

His strong jaw brushed against the side of my head with such gentleness I couldn't keep from sucking in a breath. I suspected he hadn't meant anything by the gesture, that with our proximity such touches were inevitable. Even so, I'd never been so near to a man. I found that every contact only made me more aware of him.

His hand at my waist shifted, his fingers parting as though to hold me more securely. For a second I could feel his heartbeat thudding against my back as I waited for his answer with more anticipation than I should have. Why did it matter whether Sir Aldric liked my companionship or not? Soon enough he would deliver me to Lord Pitt, and I'd likely never see him again, except perhaps at a distance.

"Does your silence mean you find my presence intolerable?" I persisted in a teasing voice even though my body was suddenly on edge.

"You are not so difficult to tolerate, my lady." His response was low and rumbling.

I expelled a breath I didn't know I'd been holding, a strange pleasure stealing through me.

"Does Lord Clearwater tolerate you?" he asked, his mouth near my ear, which only fanned the pleasure.

"Of course he more than tolerates me," I bantered. Although I'd had a fair share of suitors over the past year, including Lionel, I'd never met anyone who affected me like this man.

"Do you care for him?" Sir Aldric asked.

"He is a fine man." I forced my thoughts onto the fair-haired young Lord Clearwater who had visited several months ago. We'd seldom spoken together privately. Even if he was brusque and a rather hard man, he'd been congenial and attentive to me. He'd struck me as purposeful and determined, much like my father. "Once we spend more time together, we shall develop affection for one another."

"And pray tell what you will do if you're already betrothed to him when you discover his true nature?"

Sir Aldric's words from last night taunted me. *Lionel is a scoundrel like his father.* Truthfully, I didn't know the marquess or his son well enough to determine their character. But I had heard rumors regarding Lionel, particularly of his unfair treatment of the bondsmen in service to him.

"I suppose you are referring to the old bondsman he sent off his land because the man could no longer do the work required of him?"

"I hadn't heard that tale," Sir Aldric replied. "The stories I've heard about Lionel are not quite so tame or kind."

"You exaggerate, sir, and take pleasure in goading me."

"I would not goad you about this, my lady," he spoke in a deadly calm tone.

Even if Lionel was ruthless and calculating at times, that had nothing to do with me, did it? Besides, I was strong enough that a man like that wouldn't bend me. "My father would not consider the match if he believed I would be unhappy in it."

"He wouldn't consider it if he believed he wouldn't profit from it."

"You do not know my father."

"He seeks to increase his wealth and power in whatever way suits him."

At his harsh accusation, I stiffened and sat forward. "Your forthrightness is not welcome. I would that you refrain from speaking ill of my father."

"I hadn't taken you for a coward, my lady."

"You are correct. I am no coward."

"If you're unwilling to confront the truth and tolerate only what titillates your ears, then you're indeed a coward." His rebuke was firm and stole my response, leaving me speechless.

We rode silently as we approached the woodlands. I didn't relax back into him, and he didn't attempt to persuade me to—although part of me wished he'd apologize and endeavor to regain my favor so we could resume our camaraderie.

Instead, his body tensed. With each step we drew nearer to Bevins of Lowdown, his muscles flexed into rigid bands. A glance at him over my shoulder revealed a clenched jaw, tight set of his lips, and eyes narrowed upon the dogwood bushes.

He didn't say anything, but he'd likely sensed danger and was on high alert.

I surveyed the thick growth, the hawthorn flowers in bloom, their speckled white a contrast to the lush green. The blood-red of the honeysuckle spread in thick profusion too and would have been a pretty sight had not Sir Aldric been so tense.

He reined his steed, which snorted a hard exhale as though asking what was wrong. Sir Aldric lifted a cautioning hand to the knights behind him, and they fell silent so that the wind whistling through the gorse was a soft, sad song around us.

"My lady." Sir Aldric spoke close to my ear. "I task you with keeping your sister safe alongside Sir Darien."

"Safe?" I didn't resist as he lowered me to the ground.

Before he could answer, a cry came from one of the knights to our left. "Be alert! Incoming arrow!"

I ducked at the same time that Sir Aldric veered his horse sideways to act as a shield. I couldn't see where the arrow struck or if it hit anyone since the knights were suddenly a hive of action, preparing themselves for battle by donning their helmets and retrieving their shields. None were attired in full plate armor, but rather wore their long hauberks made of chain mail.

"Go now, my lady," Sir Aldric said more urgently. "Stay at the back of the fighting line with Sir Darien."

Already his sights were trained on a fresh volley of arrows flying in high arcs from the direction of the dogwoods.

I hurried away from the danger determined to keep Izzy out of harm's way. Dodging the knights who were spurring their horses into action, I searched frantically for my sister, finally spotting her with Sir Darien on their steeds near the supply wagons.

"Izzy!" I shouted as I wove around a wagon only to almost collide with a knight racing to the front line. Distant shouts drew closer, as the attackers poured from the forest and raced toward us. I attempted to gauge who the enemy was by the coat of arms on their attire. But from my glimpses of the men coming toward us, I saw no emblem or anything else that might indicate if they'd been sent by my father to rescue Izzy and me.

For all I knew, they were bandits who lived in the woodland and preyed upon travelers. Perhaps they'd taken stock of the wagonloads of goods and thought they could steal from Sir Aldric.

Whatever the case, I didn't wait to discover if the attackers were friend or foe. I simply had one mission and that was to shield Izzy from further distress.

Sir Darien had dismounted and was in the process of aiding Izzy from her mare when I rushed up to them. "We need to find a safe place to hide," I said.

Izzy's pale face was even whiter and her eyes wide with fright. She looked to Sir Darien for his guidance, clearly trusting that he'd find a way to protect us.

As Sir Darien gently lowered her to the ground, he scoured the chaos around us. "Over there." He pointed to a thick clump of gorse a short distance off to the side. "You'll be out of the thick of the battle there."

Holding his shield in front of us, he escorted us to the secluded spot. "Stay low," he warned, as he crouched beside us.

At the shouts and clashing of swords, I placed my arm around Izzy and huddled together, covering her body with mine. I wished I had my armor and would have felt more confident having a sword in hand.

We knelt low, attempting to keep out of sight. At a clanking, Sir Darien rose just slightly, only to have the hilt of a sword slam down onto his mail hood with a force that crumpled him to the ground.

I gasped and lunged after his sword, which had fallen a few feet away. But before I could grab it, a warrior in a peasant's cloak landed upon the sword in a lithe crouch. The move was familiar, one I'd been trained to perform.

My heart gave an irregular thump.

Even before the warrior pushed aside his hood, I saw the dark skin.

"Cecil?" I whispered as excitement renewed my strength and courage. My father had sent a rescue party just as I'd known he would.

He pressed a finger against his lips, his dark eyes assessing first me and then Izzy. With a quick glance over his shoulder, he shoved something into my hands. His gaze held mine for a long moment and filled with apology.

He rose halfway, looking again in the direction of the fighting. He tugged his hood back over his thin face and concealed his hands in the sleeves of his cloak. Then he darted away.

I moved to follow him, intending to drag Izzy along. But Cecil cast me a final glance, one that bid me to stay before he sprinted in the direction of the woods.

"Stop!" came Sir Aldric's command. I could see him running in our direction. He hesitated as if he would chase after Cecil, but then he continued charging toward us.

Dare I race after Cecil and attempt to outrun Sir Aldric? If I'd been alone without Izzy, I might have tried the feat. But even then, I would have risked capture. Besides, Cecil had clearly indicated that I should stay, that I wasn't to follow him.

I glanced down at the item he'd pressed into my hand. It appeared to be a small rolled parchment. A note.

"My lady," Aldric called as he drew near, his

handsome face a mask of concern. "Are you harmed?"

I slid the secret note out of sight through the slit of my skirt and into the pouch underneath that served as a pocket. I had no time to read it now with Sir Aldric upon us.

"We have suffered no ill," I responded as I clutched Izzy's hand and squeezed a warning. I prayed she would understand that we needed to keep Cecil's identity a secret. "But I fear Sir Darien did not fare as well."

"I saw him fall and came as fast as I could," Aldric said breathlessly, his sword drawn, his sights fixed upon Cecil who had reached the edge of the woods and disappeared into the thick growth. Cecil was well covered, his dark skin hidden. Even so, did Aldric recognize him?

A shrill whistle pierced the air, and the attackers began to retreat into the forest.

Sir Darien tossed his head and groaned.

Izzy broke away from me and crawled to his side.

"Stay here until I return for you," Aldric said tersely. He didn't wait for my reply but instead commanded his troops to pursue the attackers. With sword pointed in the direction of the forest, he charged after the retreating enemy.

My heart thudded a strange dread as I watched him surge to the front of his men and lead the pursuit. I tried to tell myself I was only worried about Cecil, that I didn't want anyone to discover his presence or to capture him. But my sights stayed upon Aldric until the forest swallowed him from view, and I had to admit I didn't want any harm to befall him either.

I stared at the woodland in the place he'd disappeared. Part of me knew I needed to make my escape with Izzy now while Aldric and most of the other knights were gone. Sir Darien was moaning and beginning to revive, but not coherent enough to stop us.

And yet, I hesitated. Cecil had bid me to stay. He could have helped us get away if that's what he'd intended.

The secret note in my pocket beckoned to me. With a sweeping glance to make sure no one was paying attention to me, I slipped my hand into my pocket and retrieved the rolled parchment. I slit the wax seal, noting it belonged to my father. Then I unrolled the paper to reveal his scrawling handwriting.

"Lord Pitt discovered the Holy Chalice on a recent raid and has it in his possession. You must find it for me. I will wait to rescue you until you have accomplished the deed."

Upon reading the instructions, I rolled up the parchment and returned it to my pocket. I would find a way later to burn the paper so no one would know of my mission.

But for now, a mixture of emotions swirled

inside me—disbelief, frustration, and even hurt that my father had placed me into this dangerous predicament. It was suddenly clear why he hadn't come to Ludlow's aid after receiving my missive regarding the attack. He'd wanted Lord Pitt to take me as prisoner so I would be in a position to steal the Holy Chalice.

Over the past few years, Father had been searching for the ancient relic since it was rumored to have curative powers. He'd heard the stories of healing from those who'd sipped wine from the cup just as the Lord did with His disciples during the Last Supper. Now he wanted the cup for Charles.

I couldn't begrudge Father's desire for Charles to be healed of his ailments. Poor Charles suffered debilitating seizures that left him weak and gasping for breath. None of the physicians Father brought in could find a way to help him, not through bloodletting, special vapors, or even expensive decoctions. Although the physicians never spoke too negatively of my brother's condition, we all realized eventually one of the seizures would kill him.

I wanted to save Charles every bit as much as my father did. I loved the young boy. And I didn't like to see him suffer.

However, was my father so partial that he was willing to sacrifice his daughters so his son could live? No wonder Cecil's eyes had been filled with an apology. If he'd had a choice, he would have rescued us rather than passing along a message.

Aldric's words from earlier pricked my conscience—the words that painted my father as a selfish man, one who thought only about himself and how he might profit.

"No," I whispered harshly. Father only wanted to save Charles. He wasn't planning to use the Holy Chalice for his own profit. And he was only calling upon me to do my duty to the family and to help save Charles.

Surely Father wouldn't ask me to search for the chalice if doing so would put me into grave danger. Likely I'd be able to locate the holy relic quickly and get word to him easily enough. Then he'd come and figure out a way to free Izzy and me.

In the meantime, I would remain Lord Pitt's unwilling prisoner.

Chapter
7

I BOWED MY HEAD TO LORD PITT. IN HIS CENTER POSITION at the head table, he was chewing upon a leg of mutton, the juice running down into his graying beard. Around him sat several of the king's advisors. The rest of the great hall was empty except for a separate table with Pitt's wife, Lady Glynnis, and her ladies.

With the retinue of knights and attendants having just returned, we would have to eat later after we unloaded the goods, took care of our mounts, and washed away the past two weeks of dust and grime.

"Windsor," Pitt said between bites. "I hear you have succeeded once again."

"Yes, my lord." I rose to my full height and met Pitt's gaze head-on. He was the only one who called me by my family name. Although he'd conceded to my desire not to reveal my identity as

Baron of Hampton, he refused to address me by a simple knight's title as everyone else did.

He was a stern man, his countenance granite. The long scar that ran from his left eye to his chin gave him a dangerous aura. But I'd learned in working for him that while he was hard and rough, he was also fair and just. He dared to do things none other in the realm would try, and because of that had won the favor of the king.

"Do you know who attacked you earlier?" Pitt asked before ripping another hunk of meat from the bone.

"No, my lord. Although I suspect it was the earl's men." I had no proof, except that our attackers had been no ordinary bandits. They'd been too skilled with their weapons and too prepared to fight. Strangely, they hadn't attempted to steal anything and only engaged us in hand-to-hand combat for a short time before retreating.

If the earl had sent them, perhaps they'd discovered they were too outnumbered to manage to free the earl's daughters. Or perhaps their surprise attack hadn't worked the way they'd hoped.

Whatever the case, we pursued them in the woods a few dozen yards before I called my men to halt. We had no reason to seek them out further since they'd taken nothing. I hadn't wanted to waste any more time in a futile chase when we were so close to Tolleymuth, Pitt's primary residence.

Besides, I'd been concerned I would have to chase down Lady Olivia. I expected that once she realized she was no longer being monitored, she'd use the opportunity to ride off with her sister. I even wondered if that was the purpose of the attack in the first place, to draw us away and give Olivia a chance to escape.

When I returned a short while later, I was surprised to discover Olivia and Isabelle were still with Sir Darien. After sparring with her in combat, I knew she was a skilled fighter who would have no trouble overcoming an injured man. But the ladies had assisted him to one of the wagon beds, and Olivia had been in the process of cleaning his head wound.

She only lifted her chin higher when I told her I hadn't expected her to be there and said, "You would have recaptured us, would you not?"

I was an excellent tracker, and indeed, I would have found her again. But the possibility of recapture hadn't stopped her from attempting to escape before. There was more to her staying than she was disclosing, but I figured I'd learn the true reason soon enough.

"Bring me the earl's daughters," Pitt said between bites. "I want to see for myself what kind of prisoners I have."

I nodded. I'd known Pitt would want to see the

women. He'd likely heard rumors regarding Olivia's beauty and desired to see for himself what kind of woman she really was.

As I exited the great hall, I was relieved to find Olivia and Isabelle sitting on the bench where I'd left them. Sir Darien stood guard on one side and Sir Perceval on the other. The presence of two guards wouldn't have stopped Olivia from fighting her way free if she'd really wanted to. Why was she behaving now after she'd given me so much trouble earlier?

"My ladies," I said with a bow. "Lord Pitt desires an audience with you."

Olivia stood and smoothed a loose strand of her hair back under the veil that she'd donned upon our arrival. I could see that she'd done her best to dislodge the dust and grime of travel. Even so, a twinge of guilt needled me that I hadn't allowed her and Isabelle to change their garments before meeting Pitt and his wife.

Of course, Olivia was as stunning as usual, with her red hair in stark contrast to her creamy skin and her beautiful green eyes, which never seemed to miss a single detail of her surroundings.

As she approached me, I couldn't stop from thinking of earlier today when she'd ridden with me, how she'd relaxed against me and we'd been able to talk freely. I'd never spoken to any woman with such ease, not even Giselle.

At times during the journey, I'd even forgotten

Olivia was supposed to be my prisoner, especially when I brushed against her. The lushness of her hair and the smooth curves of her shoulders and arms and waist had beckoned to me, awakening me to a woman's presence in a way I hadn't noticed since Giselle's death.

Part of me was beset with guilt even though Giselle had been gone for two years. Such attention to another woman felt like betrayal to the woman I'd once loved. But another part of me welcomed the rebirth of feelings toward the fairer sex. Perhaps it meant I was finally putting my past behind me.

"What does Lord Pitt plan to do with us?" Olivia asked.

I didn't exactly know, but I suspected he would be decent so long as Olivia didn't threaten him. "Lord Pitt is a hard man," I warned. "But if you do all that he asks, he will treat you fairly."

Olivia studied my face with her usual sharpness. "What will keep him from locking us into the dungeons?'

I sincerely hoped Pitt wouldn't resort to such measures. Of course, he'd shown no mercy to any of the men we'd captured over the past year and had locked them away until their families paid the required ransom. "If you respect and obey Lord Pitt, he will likely allow you to attend to his wife."

Olivia's eyes flashed with displeasure before she could hide it. I had no doubt she was familiar with the practice of ladies serving those above them. As an earl's daughter, Olivia deserved to have Lady Glynnis attend her, not the other way around.

"You must remain docile, Lady Olivia," I urged. Olivia must understand from the start that if she hoped to survive her captivity, she needed to submit to Pitt's wishes. Or he would destroy her.

I had only to picture my brother's wife, Lady Sabine, in the metal cage suspended in the tree to remember just how brutal Pitt could be when provoked. Pitt had accused Sabine of being a witch and almost burned her at the stake. He likely would have killed her, except that Bennet and I attacked his encampment and freed her.

"If you cross Lord Pitt," I said, "I cannot guarantee your safety or Isabelle's."

Olivia glanced at her sister who'd also arisen. Isabelle was decidedly more travel weary, her gown disheveled, her hair in need of grooming. Worry rippled over Olivia's lovely features before she forced cool impassivity into her expression.

"You may take me to your master," Olivia announced.

I hesitated, suddenly wishing I could whisk the two sisters away someplace safe, away from Pitt, away from their father, away from the political intrigue that held them captive. But I was the one responsible for bringing them here. And now that I'd done the deed, I would have to ensure that no harm befell them.

Fighting the heaviness in my heart, I led the women into the great hall, down the long center aisle to the head table where Pitt was washing his greasy fingers in a silver ewer a servant held out to him.

"My lord," I said, "I present the Earl of Ulster's daughters, Lady Olivia and Lady Isabelle."

Both curtsied prettily before Pitt.

As Olivia rose, I caught sight of the disdain on her face before she could mask it. From the narrowing of Pitt's eyes, I guessed he'd seen it as well.

The women at the adjacent table had ceased their discourse and were watching the prisoners with interest. Lady Glynnis was a hefty, large-boned woman with a round face. Her eyes and nose and mouth were small amidst the mounds of her flesh. As if to make up for her lack of natural beauty, she adorned herself in the most ostentatious of costumes, elaborate headdresses, voluminous jewelry, and lavish gowns.

I'd noted at other times and heard rumors among the married knights, that Lady Glynnis was easily provoked by any woman she deemed prettier than herself. Perhaps it was for the best that Olivia and Isabelle hadn't had time to refresh themselves. Hence forward, I would need to warn them to dress plainly and try not to attract undue attention.

"Lady Olivia." Pitt wiped his hands on the towel his servant provided. He deliberately dried each finger slowly before raising the towel to his mouth and beard and wiping away the remains of his meal, all without taking his hard gaze from Olivia. "I bid you and your sister welcome to Tolleymuth."

Olivia's shoulders were rigid with defiance. I silently willed her to refrain from retorting with something rude. I wasn't sure why I cared so much that she behave. I'd already warned her. If she chose to ignore my admonitions, that was her fault. She'd get what she deserved.

But did she truly deserve this? Any of it?

I banished the question and forced myself to remain alert.

"Lord Pitt," Olivia said in her usual direct tone. "We both know that my welcome here is contingent upon my father. But I do thank you for the kindness your men have shown to me and my sister during our ordeal. I commend them for the honorable way they have treated us. It speaks well of you and the manner in which you run your household."

Olivia's response surprised me. And from the widening of Pitt's eyes, I could tell it had surprised him as well.

He regarded her a moment before answering, as though testing the sincerity of her words. "I do not deserve the praise you bestow upon me, Lady Olivia. Any gratitude for kindness must be given to my captain, for he is a man of honor."

Pitt nodded in my direction, but Lady Olivia kept her attention focused on him.

"Windsor," he said, "is the finest man I know. But I am not so fine. Rather I am . . ."

Ruthless. Determined. Dangerous. I silently filled in the blank. Pitt wasn't someone I wished to face on the battlefield again. However, after my time in his servitude, I'd learned he was also reasonable and ultimately sought to do what was right, even if his methods at times were harsh.

"I'm interested in ensuring the king's well-being," he continued with a glance at the king's advisors who were watching the proceedings with obvious interest. "I try to do what is necessary for the greater good of the kingdom."

"I respect your loyalty to the king, my lord," she replied. "Hopefully you will respect mine to my family."

Pitt remained silent for a long moment. The clanging of pots and the voices of servants in the kitchen wafted into the room. Finally, Pitt picked up the goblet that remained on the table before him, took several gulps. "I can see that you are a strong woman. And although I should lock you up, I shall give you the chance to serve my wife."

"Thank you, my lord." She bowed her head.

"It will not go well for you if you make me regret my decision." His words rang with ominous warning.

Olivia nodded but didn't meet his gaze.

I should feel pleased by the outcome of the meeting, for it meant Olivia and her sister would live in relative comfort during their stay at Tolleymuth.

But I felt only trepidation as if somehow Pitt and I had been sucked into a scheme that we knew nothing about. I could only pray Olivia would heed my advice and remain meek and cooperative during her stay. Otherwise, I didn't know if I'd be able to save her from Pitt's wrath.

"And you should also know," Pitt added, "my scribe has written to your father letting him know he has one month starting from today to pay the ransom and sign a letter declaring his loyalty to the king. After that, I will punish him even further."

From the sharp edge of Pitt's tone, I knew he'd do whatever he needed in order to bring the earl into submission. One month wasn't long, but the earl should have no trouble accumulating the amount he owed Pitt. The question was whether he'd be willing to pledge himself to the king and cease his plotting with other Marcher lords. Did he care enough for his daughters and their freedom to give up his rebellious ways? Or would he sacrifice them for his own selfish desires?

I prayed for Olivia and Isabelle's sakes that their father was as devoted as Olivia believed.

Chapter 8

I peered down the long hallway both ways to make sure I was unnoticed before I slid into the chapel and closed the door behind me.

After a week at Tolleymuth as a servant to Lord Pitt's wife, I wasn't sure I had the patience to go another hour, much less another day or week. Lady Glynnis had been jealous and petty and demeaning all week, finding fault with everything I did.

Her demanding schedule made searching for the Holy Chalice nearly impossible. She woke us all well before dawn to pray with her. Then after breaking our fast with plain porridge and hot milk, we prayed again in the chapel.

Finally, when we returned to the great hall, Lady Glynnis would gather us all into a sunny corner where we would sit on stools and embroider for hours. Mostly we worked on new gowns for Lady Glynnis, sewing colorful stitches and tiny seed pearls in embroidered flowers along the hem, on sleeves, and at the front of skirts.

As a young girl, I'd only learned the most basic stitches, having spent most of my time practicing sword drills and fighting maneuvers with Cecil. Thus my needlework was of poor quality, and Lady Glynnis took pleasure in using her silver scissors to rip out sections of my needlework and tasking me to do it over.

"Only the best," she'd say as she cut the uneven threads and sent the pearls cascading in all directions over the floor. "The stitches must be flawless."

A time or two, I'd almost thrown the fabric into Lady Glynnis's face and stomped away. But a glance at Isabelle sewing contentedly with the other ladies had stopped my rashness. With the sunshine turning Isabelle's hair into spun gold and highlighting the healthy pink in her cheeks, I'd shoved aside my frustrations and quelled my anger.

Lord Pitt's warning was never far from my mind. *It will not go well for you if you make me regret my decision.* I'd sensed he wasn't a man of idle threats, that he planned to follow through on everything he'd spoken. He would punish me if I defied him. And he would punish me if Father didn't negotiate with him by the end of the month.

The problem was that Father wouldn't do anything until I brought him the Holy Chalice. But how could I search for the ancient relic when Lady Glynnis kept me busy at every hour of the day?

Even now as I breathed in the spicy waft of incense that permeated the chapel, I knew Lady Glynnis would begin to wonder where I was and why I was taking so long to relieve myself.

I strode to the front of the chapel, to the altar. The priest often provided the Eucharist from supplies stored within the altar. Perhaps he'd placed the Holy Chalice with the other elements used for distributing the Lord's Supper.

The embroidered linen that graced the altar draped over the back, concealing the open shelves. I glanced at the chapel door, then bent to investigate, pushing aside the covering and taking in the assortment of wine bottles, cups, and platters. There were rosaries and crucifixes and more embroidered linens. But there was no Holy Chalice—which I knew to be distinct from others by its simplicity and the engraving of a lamb at its center.

At the click of the door and the movement of the handle, I rounded the altar and bounded toward the closest prayer cushion. The door swung wide before I could fall to a kneeling position.

Sir Aldric. Upon seeing him, I ceased my frantic pretense. Dressed as usual in his chain mail hauberk, he made a forbidding picture filling the doorway with his broad shoulders, bulky arms, and hand upon the hilt of his sword at his belt.

Since our arrival to Tolleymuth and his warnings to me before I'd met Lord Pitt, we hadn't conversed again. I'd seen him at a distance, usually at meal times. While I sat with Lady Glynnis at the women's table, he ate several tables away with the other knights of his rank. But he never even so much as glanced my way, not even in passing.

Though he conversed with the men around him, he was never talkative or loud, never purposefully attracting attention, always modest and humble.

Yet, his presence in the great hall was commanding, and he drew the attention of the few unmarried women at my table. With his rugged good looks, dark hair and eyes, and the strength of his bearing, he was easily the handsomest man there. The maidens boldly watched him and coyly flirted. I was secretly pleased he paid them no heed and seemed oblivious to their charm.

A time or two, I willed him to glance at me, to acknowledge my presence, to remember the brief closeness we'd shared during the ride here.

But perhaps the proximity during our travels hadn't affected him the same way it had me.

Besides, I told myself, he wasn't my concern. He was a servant of Lord Pitt sent to do a job. With the task completed, he was free of any obligation to me.

Now, as he stood in the chapel doorway, his presence was overpowering as usual. He radiated strength and purpose. And of course, he was still handsome with strands of his windblown hair loose from the leather strip, his jaw shadowed with unshaven stubble, and his dark eyes framed by long lashes.

He opened his mouth to speak, but then with a fleeting look into the hallway, he closed the door first. "My lady," he whispered, his hand against the handle, his gaze settling on me. "You'll arouse suspicion by wandering in here by yourself."

"I have come to pray." I looked pointedly at the prayer cushion. "There is no crime in that, is there?"

"We both know you aren't in here to pray."

"You presume to know my intentions?"

"I know you are seeking after something, though I don't yet know what."

His sharp assessment of the truth took me by surprise. How could he possibly know I'd been searching when he never looked at me? Or was he spying on me when I didn't realize it? "I did not think you remembered I still existed, and yet somehow you seem intimately acquainted with my every movement."

"As Lord Pitt's captain of the guard, I make it my business to know everything that goes on behind the castle walls."

"Surely you have no need to concern yourself with a meager prisoner such as myself."

Sir Aldric released the handle and took a step away from the door. "Meager prisoner? You surely don't think so little of yourself. That would be out of character."

His words, though spoken evenly, grated my pride like the sharp prongs of a wool carder.

I left my place by the prayer cushion and started down the aisle toward him. "Then you believe I am vain, Captain?" How dare he!

He watched me draw near. I had no weapons I could use to attack him. I greatly missed my custom-made sword and my dagger. And I hadn't found anything else lying around that I might confiscate to use as a makeshift weapon. I could only fight with my hands and sharp tongue, and I aimed to do my best with both.

I stopped in front of him, my gaze daring him to insult me again so that I might slap him this time.

Likewise, his eyes challenged me and refused to back down.

"Should I take your silence to mean that you

despise me?" I finally asked, not sure why it should matter what he thought about me. Sir Aldric wasn't my concern. Even so, my breath snagged in my chest as I awaited his response.

"I don't despise you, my lady."

"But neither do you like me."

He hesitated, shifting his strong frame.

His indecision cut me. Most men admired me and told me how beautiful I was. I should take satisfaction with the adulation I'd already so easily garnered. Why then did I long for his? He was only one man among many.

Yet even as I tried again to dismiss the insecurities, I realized I longed for his respect and admiration because he was a man of honor. Respect and admiration meant so much more when they came from someone who lived out the qualities.

"If I despised and disliked you, my lady," he finally said in a low tone. "I wouldn't be in here at this moment attempting to keep you from an action you might later regret."

Something in his eyes sent a warm streak through my insides, something that wound around me and tied itself up so that I didn't want to move and instead longed to stand near him and bask in the sensation.

"Do you ever do things you might later regret?" I asked. "Or are you always honorable?"

"We make hard choices every day," he

responded studying my face. "And sometimes in hindsight, we wish we could undo a choice and make a different decision."

"Then you can understand I have hard choices to make."

"The consequences may prove too difficult to bear."

Was he thinking of the choices he'd made after his wife had died, the ruination he'd caused his family and home?

"If Lord Pitt discovers you're conspiring against him in any way, he'll make you suffer." Sir Aldric's brows slanted above eyes that were warm with concern. "I have no wish to see you suffer."

The candlelight from the altar flickered across his features, highlighting the strength in his chin, the firmness of his mouth, the solidness of his jaw. "If you are concerned, then why do you not look at me or speak to me when we are in the great hall together?"

My question was completely off-topic and much too bold, but it was out before I could drag it back in.

His eyes registered a moment of surprise. "I keep to my place, my lady. I don't wish to overstep the boundaries and set a poor example to the other knights under my command. If I promote a familiarity with you, then my men may imitate me."

"Or they may not care."

"I've already rebuked some of my men for speaking about you. And I have no desire for others to look at you and do the same."

"Of what ill do they speak?"

"No ill." His voice dropped a notch. "They speak only of your beauty."

"Oh?" I watched his expression and attempted to decipher his thoughts. "Surely you would not judge them too harshly?"

His lips curled into a slight but rueful smile. "I would flog them if I could."

At his admission, my own smile broke free, and a strange delight pooled in my belly. Was he jealous when the other men spoke of me or paid me attention?

"If you are punishing your men, then it must be because they are speaking falsehoods and imagining beauty where there is none. You are a cruel master." I was unabashedly pushing him for a compliment, but I couldn't seem to stop myself.

He took a step toward me so that he stood a mere handbreadth away. I was suddenly aware of the span of his broad chest, his clean musky scent, and the heat that emanated from his body.

Although he was taller, the intense glimmer in his eyes seemed to draw me upward and into him farther. The pull was irresistible. Every nerve sparked at his nearness, charged with the need for a connection with him. I waited for him to slip a hand around my back and pull me against him, or at the very least to caress my cheek.

But he initiated no move to touch me. Instead he made a languid pastime of studying my features, his breath echoing in the space between us.

"My lady," he whispered, finally settling his sights upon my lips. "If my men speak falsehoods, it is only because they don't do your beauty justice."

The compliment was more than I ever could have dreamed or expected. And it left me too breathless to speak. I wanted to fall into his arms and have him sweep me up, but I was too overcome with pleasure to move.

Before I could give in to the desire to swoon against him, he broke our connection by pivoting and opening the door. In an instant, he'd retreated into the hallway. He bowed his head at me in a gesture of servitude. Then he turned and strode away.

I was helpless but to watch him, wanting to call him back but knowing with certainty that this man was not at my beckoning. I had thought to play with him, to coax him into flattering me. But he'd easily shown me, as he had every other time we'd interacted, he was the one in control and I wouldn't be able to manipulate him.

I sagged against the doorframe, suddenly weak from the interaction with him. I clung to the cold stone to keep from collapsing.

For the first time in my life, I'd met a man who neither feared me nor bowed to my wishes. And I liked it.

Chapter 9

I SPUN IN A SEMICIRCLE ARC, PARRIED A COUNTERATTACK, and then lunged, putting all my strength behind the next attack.

My opponent fell back a step, not expecting my heavy swing. I followed up my lunge with a series of continuous sharp blows against the other knight's sword until at last he stumbled and fell backward. He landed on the ground, his sword spinning out of reach.

I pressed the tip of my blade at his gorget and held it there for several seconds. Then I broke away, sheathed my sword, and strode to the side of the corded-off fighting ring. Once there, I removed my helmet.

From the corner of my eye, I caught sight of my opponent rising and flexing his hand which was likely sore from my attack. He too removed his helmet, revealing the sweat that rolled down his forehead and cheeks.

The heat from the June afternoon had grown oppressive, even more so within the confines of our armor. The grit of dust mingled with my own perspiration, and I could taste the salt of it on my tongue.

"Well done, Windsor," Pitt called from where he sat under a canopied pavilion in the shade while servants stirred a breeze by pumping large fans. "You remain our undefeated champion."

I bowed in acknowledgement of his praise. The tournament had been ongoing for the past several days with knights coming from the surrounding lands to participate. I'd sincerely hoped the tournament would draw the Earl of Ulster, that among the throngs of other lords and ladies, he'd feel safer delivering the ransom to Pitt.

But with the tournament coming to a close, I'd resigned myself to the possibility that the earl wasn't planning to ransom his daughters. That likelihood frightened me more than I cared to admit.

Though I refrained from glancing past Lady Glynnis to the bench where the lowliest of the ladies had been relegated, I knew Olivia was still sitting in the same spot next to Isabelle where she'd been before my fight had commenced.

She'd taken her place there whenever Lady Glynnis came out to the lists to watch the tournament. Although Olivia had done her best to remain a passive onlooker, I'd noticed the longing in her eyes to be one of the privileged allowed to fight. She watched each round with keen interest, following moves with practiced skill, her fingers twitching with the need for a sword.

Someone had foolishly indulged Olivia's whims as a child by teaching her swordfighting. While I understood the benefit in learning self-defense, I saw no other reason for ladies to engage in physical combat. It was simply too dangerous. Even if Olivia was bored with the embroidery she was forced to do every day with Lady Glynnis, such work was much more suited to a lady.

"You'll have the place of honor at the banquet this eve," Pitt declared as he rose to his feet. "And you'll choose one of the fair maidens to accompany you." He swept his arm over the unmarried ladies who cooled themselves with elegantly decorated folding fans.

I swept a cursory glance over the women without seeing any of them. I had no desire to have a dinner companion, having no wish to mislead any of the young maidens into believing I was interested when I was not. But Pitt would insist as he had at past tournaments.

After one of my previous championships during the feasting, Pitt had encouraged me to take a wife from among the maidens. After much teasing and cajoling, I'd divulged to him that I had no desire or plans to wed again. Once had been enough for me. I'd failed in my efforts to love Giselle the way she'd needed. If I'd been a better husband, if I'd loved her the way she'd needed, then maybe she wouldn't have died.

I wasn't worthy of loving again. I was better off by myself.

Though Pitt was well aware of my feelings on the matter and now understood what had driven me into his debt, he still pushed women at me all too often. He was good-natured, even fatherly about it. He had no children of his own, only two married daughters from Lady Glynnis's first husband. At twenty-two, I was half his age, the age of a son if he'd had one. Since he regarded me as a son, he'd designed to help me overcome my past whether or not I wanted his aid.

"Who will the lucky woman be this time, Windsor?" Pitt called exuberantly, giving me no choice but to pick someone.

I let my sights drift to the women again, this time studying them more carefully. In their bright garments, frilly veils, and excessive ribbons, I had a difficult time focusing on their faces. Lady Glynnis, the most extravagantly attired of them all, smiled and inclined her head toward Lady Beatrice, the daughter of one of her closest friends, who sat demurely beside her. Lady Beatrice had been living at Tolleymuth for the past month. She'd attempted to engage my attention on numerous occasions, but I'd ignored her just as I had all the others.

If I chose her as my partner for the evening's festivities, would I only encourage her affection? But how could I graciously decline Lady Glynnis's subtle directive? Should I pretend I hadn't seen her nod?

From my peripheral, I could tell Olivia was watching me with undisguised interest, waiting to see which of the women caught my attention.

My thoughts strayed to the chapel where I'd encountered her earlier in the week. Unbeknownst to her, I'd watched her slip away from the sewing circle and had followed her to the chapel. I'd suspected she was searching for something, and her rummaging behind the altar had proven my suspicions true.

I'd planned to only admonish her to cease her clandestine searches. If Pitt learned she was sneaking around the castle, he'd discipline her and show her no mercy. And strangely I'd found myself repelled by the prospect of further harm befalling Olivia or her sister. After all, I'd already caused them enough danger by bringing them to Tolleymuth.

With her well-being utmost on my mind, I'd entered the chapel intending to warn her. And somehow, she'd unwittingly drawn me in. I'd fallen prey to her charm and beauty, even if only for a moment.

Why do you not look at me or speak to me when we are in the great hall together? Her question had been low and intimate and had sparked like flint in my blood. She'd desired my flattery, saw my aloofness as a challenge, needed to add me to the long list of men who worshipped her.

I hadn't told her that I did look at her—often. Instead, I'd attempted to rebuff her questions. But somehow in the end, she'd wrested the words she'd wanted to hear from me anyway. As I'd walked away, I'd vowed to do better at keeping my distance from her.

She was a temptation I didn't need, making me wish all the more fervently the earl would submit to the king and Pitt's demands so he could take his daughters home where they belonged.

Was there nothing more we could do to entice the earl to hasten his arrival? The sooner he came the better, not only for my sanity, but for their safety. Once the month deadline passed, Pitt would increase the pressure upon the earl. And I dreaded to think of what Pitt might decide to do to one or both of the sisters.

What if I picked Olivia to be my partner for the evening? Would word reach her father and alarm him? If he believed a lowly knight like myself was interested in his daughter, would he claim her more readily to avoid losing the match he planned with Lionel Lacy?

"My lord," I said, facing Pitt again. "May I have a word alone?"

Pitt waved me over and at the same time,

those who'd gathered around him backed away to give us a modicum of privacy.

"What is it, Windsor?" he chortled. "You know you may have any woman you choose. They all adore you."

"And you know I have no desire for any," I said quietly.

His grin only widened, tightening the long white scar that ran the length of his profile. "You may continue to punish yourself for your past, but that doesn't mean you are a cold-blooded man who has no desires."

I started to protest, but then decided against it. My interactions with Olivia had shown that my desires could still be awakened, even against my will. Perhaps my plan to choose her for the evening was unwise and would only stir feelings better left untouched.

"Give the women a chance, Windsor, and in so doing give yourself another opportunity at happiness too."

"Very well," I said resignedly, knowing he wouldn't be satisfied until I agreed with him. "Since you have my goodwill at heart and wish only for my happiness, will you allow me the opportunity to spend equal time with all the maidens? Then I need not single out only one but will have the chance to interact with everyone."

Pitt's smile fell away, and he regarded me with a hard, knowing glint. "Is this one more attempt to avoid forming an attachment, Windsor?"

In some ways, he was right. Keeping the exchanges with each maiden brief wouldn't allow for deeper connections. On the other hand, I could appease him by agreeing to make the most of the evening. "I vow I shall do my best to give the women a chance, as you've requested."

Pitt studied me a moment. "Good." Then with a nod, he stood and raised his hand to garner the attention of the gathering. "The captain of my guard and my champion knight has decided he will give all the maidens equal attention during the feast and dance tonight. And when the eve is over, he will narrow down his favorite ladies who will then be in the running to become his bride."

At once the air was filled with gasps and murmurs of excitement.

"My lord," I protested, a surge of panic rising swiftly and threatening to drown me. "You misunderstood my intentions."

The clamor around us only intensified, and when Pitt glanced at me, his smile was too innocent. "You've given the people something to look forward to, Windsor."

"I agreed to give the maidens a chance," I growled, "not pick a bride."

Pitt clamped me on the shoulder affectionately. "If you fulfill your vow, I guarantee you'll be married before summer's end."

I shook my head. Pitt could scheme all he

wanted, but he wouldn't move me. I had no intention of getting married by summer's end or ever.

He'd discover that soon enough.

I reclined in the steaming tub of water, letting the warm water wash away the grime of the tournament. The long streaks of pink in the fading sky outside my chamber window told me the dreaded eve would soon be upon me.

Every time one of my squires opened my chamber door, the aromas of roasted quail, custards and jams, and herb-glazed vegetables breezed inside and reminded me of the coming feast as well.

I'd tired of the excited thrum my men couldn't hide and had dismissed them to attend to their own grooming. I hoped their absence would give me a few moments of peace. Yet as time slipped away, any semblance of peace I'd found slipped away as well.

If only I could create a viable excuse to skip the festivities. If only I'd paid better attention to Pitt's scheming and hadn't trapped myself into picking a bride.

Why would any of the ladies want me anyway? None knew my true status as Baron of Hampton.

To them, I was merely a landless knight without a title. They'd likely heard of the wealth I'd accumulated over the year in working for Pitt. And of course, they fancied me a hero for winning the championship today.

But those things were superficial. If a woman was attracted to me for such qualities, then she was shallow, and I didn't want a shallow relationship. Actually, I didn't want any kind of relationship. Not shallow. Not deep. Not any.

With a long sigh, I slipped further down into my bath, submerging my head so the water would wash away the sweat and dust in my hair. Through the bubbles in my ears, I heard the door to my chamber open. It moved too slowly and cautiously to be any of my men.

For a moment, I kept myself submerged and then soundlessly surfaced. While the tub wasn't as enormous as the one Pitt used, I'd been given a good-sized one, and it covered me entirely while still allowing some room to move around.

In fact, Pitt had been more than generous, giving me one of the largest chambers among the guest rooms to live in rather than relegating me to the barracks where the majority of knights and squires bunked. Although the furnishings were simple, I had a large canopied bed, a writing table and chair, a wardrobe, and several other smaller pieces of furniture. The walls were whitewashed and without décor, but the simplicity suited me.

My squires slept among the rushes on the floor, ready to serve me at a moment's notice, all good men who worked and fought hard.

The door closed softly. A soft tread told me someone was in the room. Someone light and lithe. Certainly not one of my squires. Most likely a young servant.

I started to lift my head to alert the servant to my presence. But I suddenly had the feeling the young servant was an intruder, sneaking through my room.

I held myself motionless and listened as the footsteps crossed in the direction of one of the chests where I stored my share of the treasures I took during the raids. The two I kept in my chamber were nearly full, which meant I was due for a trip home sometime in the near future so I could add to Maidstone's coffers.

Bennet and Sabine were still living there, but Bennet had let me know on my last visit that he planned to travel at summer's end to Sabine's home and stay there with her grandmother during the winter months. In the most recent missive, I'd detected Bennet's desire that I return to my place as Baron of Hampton so he and Sabine could move to her home permanently. But I hadn't replied to Bennet. I didn't want to tell him I wasn't ready to live at Maidstone, that maybe I never would be. I hoped over time, he'd figure that out on his own.

I remained silent and still, breathing quietly and

listening to the intruder reach one of the chests. The quiet rattle of the chain and lock told me the intruder was attempting to steal from me.

I poked my head up, but before I could see over the rim, I sank back into the water. The thief could try all he wanted to open the chests, but the keys were well hidden, secure. He wouldn't find treasure here in my chambers, rather only disappointment.

Was it one of the guests? Or perhaps one of Pitt's servants?

My squires had taken away my clothing, wet and sour with sweat. My clean garments for the evening were folded neatly on the floor with a towel next to my weapons. They'd polished my sword and dagger and had placed them on the floor within easy reach. I'd have to jump from the tub, grab my weapons, and attack all in one move, preferably before the intruder realized I was in the room.

Another clanking of the chain informed me the thief was still meddling with the lock. Was he attempting to pick it open? At a decisive click and the moan of the chest lid rising, I stiffened in surprise.

The thief was skilled.

My plan of attack suddenly required more caution than I'd anticipated.

Carefully, I lifted my head and peeked over the edge of the tub.

A woman with long red hair stood at the chest with her back facing me. However, I didn't need to see her face to recognize her at once.

Olivia. Handling her would require a different tactic altogether.

Chapter
10

I grazed my fingers over the mounds of jewels and silver coins. The chest was filled to the brim with countless items—tasseled pillows, silk blankets, embroidered tapestries, parchment manuscripts, and even a number of paintings.

How had Sir Aldric gained such wealth? Was this his payment? His share of the profits from ransacking Lord Pitt's enemies?

I dug my fingers through the jewels but stilled at the sight of a circular gold brooch studded with emeralds. My mother's brooch, the one I'd knelt to retrieve from my jewelry chest before we'd been captured. In my haste to defend Cecil from Sir Aldric and his men, I'd neglected to hide the key again.

My stomach roiled at the foolishness of my mistake. But the bitter acid rapidly changed to anger. Although Aldric and his men had every right to take my jewelry as the spoils of war, my indignation swelled anyway.

At the slight whisper of a sound, I glanced toward the door. I didn't know how long I had before anyone suspected I hadn't gone to the great hall with the other women. And I didn't know if Sir Aldric would be returning to his room before the feast.

Before entering his chambers, I'd waited a short distance away in a small alcove until I'd heard the men leave. I'd chanced a glance at their retreating forms and had waited several minutes to make sure everyone was gone before braving entry into Sir Aldric's chambers.

After searching almost every other room in the castle during the past two weeks, I'd yet to look into his. I hadn't investigated Lord Pitt's private chambers either. And time was running out. The month was half over, and I hadn't seen the Holy Chalice anywhere.

What if Father had been wrong about Lord Pitt having the sacred relic?

I returned my attention to the chest in front of me. I wouldn't know if he'd been wrong until I completed my exploration, which meant taking advantage of the few minutes I had to scour Sir Aldric's chambers.

I grabbed the brooch and shoved it through the layers of my skirt to my pocket when a voice from behind stopped me.

"My lady," said a calm but calculated voice. "What a pleasant surprise."

Sir Aldric?

My pulse startled, tripping and tumbling within my chest. When I'd peeked into his chambers, I'd been careful to scan the entirety before entering. Had he been hiding somewhere?

With heated resolve, I spun to face him. On the opposite side of his bed, he reclined in a large wooden tub. When I'd glanced at the tub before, I'd assumed it was empty.

However, from the way his wet hair was plastered to his face and neck along with the water droplets on his bare shoulders, I guessed he'd been there all along, likely submerged.

"I did not realize you were here, sir." I said the first thing that came to mind.

"Clearly." He reclined casually. His bronzed arms were stretched in relaxed fashion over the back of the tub revealing not only his bare shoulders but also the upper half of his chest.

His very bare chest.

I was paralyzed and could only stare at his glistening flesh, the sculpted muscles that rippled with restrained power. I'd never seen a man in a state of undress, not even in the least form. Though I should have been scandalized, I was more fascinated than afraid.

"I'm always relieved to discover I'm pleasant

to look upon." He combed his fingers through his wet hair, causing his bicep to bulge.

I swallowed hard, knowing I should look away, but unable to tear my gaze from him.

"Even though you're enjoying the show, I cannot indulge you any longer." He unfolded a nearby towel and started to rise.

I gasped and spun around so rapidly I tangled in my skirt, tripped, and fell against the open chest. Heat spilled into my face and mortification seeped into every pore. I wanted nothing more than to run from the room and hide in embarrassment.

But at the sloshing of water followed by the slap of feet against the floor, I gasped again, gripped the edge of the chest, and closed my eyes tightly. Although he was well behind me and I couldn't see anything now, just the knowledge that he was clad only in a towel made me want to slink through the cracks into the floorboards.

As he padded away from the tub, I held myself motionless, hardly daring to breathe. The rub of wool against flesh told me he was drying himself. A second later, the rasp of linen over damp skin was the sign he was dressing himself.

I waited, praying he would hurry.

"So, my lady." He finally broke the silence. The clank of metal indicated he was donning his weapon belt. "If you aren't in my chamber to watch me finish my bath, then why are you here?"

There was something hard in his tone, something that warned me I needed to leave now. But I was still too afraid to move, afraid if I turned I'd find him only half-dressed.

"I made a mistake. I should not have come in." I took a deep breath, desperately trying to find a plausible excuse for why I was in his chambers breaking into his locked chest.

His bare feet plodded across the rushes toward me.

I tensed. I'd gotten myself into deep trouble, and this time I knew no way out.

He halted behind me. At the heat of his presence, my mind flashed with the image of his sculpted shoulders and chest.

I'd thought him winsome when I'd watched him fight in the tournament. He'd been daring and skilled and ruggedly appealing. I'd understood the amorous way the other women had gawked at him and why he'd caught their fancy. Not only was he a champion fighter, but he was entirely too handsome for anyone's good.

With the wealth and power Lord Pitt bestowed upon him, he was a prize catch for many of the maidens still waiting for matches, although certainly not appropriate for a woman of my status.

He stood unmoving behind me, close enough I could hear his breathing and feel its warmth at the back of my neck.

I waited for him to speak or spin me around and demand to know what I was doing there. But he waited too.

The tension mounted. It was strangely charged, the air fairly crackling with something I couldn't name. It reminded me of the time we'd been alone in the chapel.

When his fingers grazed my hip, I didn't resist the touch. In fact, I found that I basked in the feel of him. His hand spread, his fingers splaying in that almost possessive hold he'd used when I'd ridden with him.

I was tempted to take a step backward and let him fold me against his chest. I could picture myself leaning my head against his shoulder and him pressing his nose into my hair.

His hand slipped lower. Before I knew what he was doing, his fingers darted through the slit in my skirt into my pocket. He jerked his hand loose and stepped away.

My pocket felt suddenly lighter and I knew why. He'd pilfered my mother's brooch.

I pivoted and lunged after his hand, intending to take back what belonged to me. But he dangled the brooch above our heads out of my reach.

"I see that you're not only skilled at sword-play but at thievery as well." His eyes glinted like the sharp tip of a dagger.

I groped after the brooch again, angry at him for manipulating me so that he could take it back and angry at myself for nurturing any sort of attraction to him. Why did I so easily fall into the role of a simpering spineless maiden whenever he drew nigh?

He held the brooch higher, so much so that I wouldn't be able to grasp it unless I climbed up his torso. Although he wore only his first layer of clothing, at least it was something, and I could shed my mortification from before.

"Give it back to me," I demanded.

"I have every right to cut off your hand for stealing from me." Before I could react, his knife was out and the blade pressed against my sleeve.

I ceased my struggling. I was in a precarious situation, and I'd clearly lost the tenuous trust and respect I'd gained with him. Although he was a fierce man, he wasn't a brute, and I knew he wouldn't cut off my hand. But he would sever the bond that had grown between us and cut me out of his life, and I didn't want that to happen, though I could not say why.

"I did not steal from you," I stated firmly.

"I witnessed you breaking into my chest and taking this brooch." His voice was hard and the knife against my wrist unyielding.

"I cannot steal something that already belongs to me." I met his gaze with a fierce one of my own. "In fact, if anyone deserves to have his hand cut off for thieving, it should be you."

His expression was unreadable, and his eyes still glinted with steel.

"You stole my mother's brooch, my most prized jewel," I said.

The pressure of the knife lessened.

"My mother said it was her favorite jewel because the emeralds were as beautiful as my eyes."

He dropped the knife but continued to hold the brooch as well as my gaze.

Suddenly I was conscious again of his nearness and the heat that crackled between us, and my stomach twirled a wild dance step.

What was it about this man that turned my mind into a bowl of mush? I ought to plan my next move or at least find an excuse with which to free myself from this predicament. But all I could think about was how deep and dark and beautiful his eyes were.

"My lady," he whispered, his voice thick.

"Yes?" I whispered in return, surprised by the eagerness in my tone.

"I am no fool. You may have located this brooch. But it isn't what you came here for or what you have been seeking these past days."

His astuteness, as usual, startled me, but I forced myself to remain just as calm as he appeared to be. If he could stay unmoved by my close proximity, then I had to learn to do the same with him. How was it that he could affect me so thoroughly, but my presence had no sway over him?

I shifted my attention to the shirt clinging to his chest. I boldly tugged at the linen, so that it pulled loose. Then I straightened the fabric at the shoulder as if such an intimate gesture was normal between us.

Finally, I took a step back, still saying nothing, for I could speak no words in my defense. When he didn't detain me, I moved several more steps toward the door. I wanted to make my getaway before he could say or do anything else that would reveal how much power he had over me.

I only managed another step when his hand circled my arm and stopped me. The touch wasn't forceful or angry as it had been before. And when I met his gaze again, I was relieved to see the sharp glint was gone.

He pressed something hard into my palm. "Your mother was wrong. The emeralds are not nearly as beautiful as your eyes."

As he released me and I continued across the room, I realized what he'd given me: my mother's brooch along with another reason to like him more than I should.

Chapter 11

I WAS WEARY OF THE ATTENTION AND WEARY OF THE women. For the life of me, I couldn't remember why I'd ever agreed to spend time equally with each of the maidens during the feasting and dancing.

After yet another dance, I slipped into my place of honor next to Pitt at the head table. He broke away from his conversation with the lord opposite him and turned to me, an eager grin making his scarred face look younger.

"Any of the fair maidens catch your eye yet?" he asked too loudly so that the conversation at the women's table died away. "And have you danced with all of them?"

I wanted to cringe at the interest now directed my way, but I masked my irritation with a smile, especially when I caught Olivia watching me with a slight smirk. She'd dined at Lady Glynnis's table but clearly separate from the others. While the ladies had dressed up for the occasion, Olivia and Isabelle wore their everyday gowns, one of the two garments they'd been allowed to keep from among the many that had been taken from them during the raid.

I suspected Pitt would give the rest of their garments to Lady Glynnis, and she would eventually make them over into new more elaborate gowns for herself.

Even so, Olivia and Isabelle were as beautiful as always. And I found myself wishing for just one dance with Olivia. Although she was a prisoner, she was still one of the ladies, and I had made a declaration to give them all equal time, hadn't I?

"Well?" Pitt asked again. "Have you danced with all the eligible maidens?"

"Almost all." I reached for my goblet and took a swig. A new lively tune filled the great hall as well as the laughter and chatter of the many guests. The air was heavy with the scents of the sweet delicacies, the marzipans, tarts, and custards, all baked golden to perfection.

Although the shutters on the many long windows throughout the hall had been opened to allow in the coolness of the night, the crowded banquet hall had grown warm.

Pitt studied the women's table, likely taking note of the ladies who were making eyes and smiling at me.

I lowered my lashes and watched Olivia as I did from time to time without her knowing I was doing so. My thoughts returned to earlier in the eve when she'd snuck into my chambers during my bath.

I'd accused her of stealing when I'd been guilty of the same. I had indeed taken her most prized possessions. Of course, at the time of my invasion of Ludlow Castle, I'd justified my actions by telling myself the items were spoils of war, that the earl deserved the losses, that I was exacting justice against crimes committed in the realm.

But did I really have the right to take everything that had belonged to Olivia?

"You're staring at Lady Olivia again," Pitt said dipping his spoon into a silver bowl filled with creamy custard.

"No I'm not."

Pitt barked a laugh. "You can't fool me. I see the way you watch her. Now go ask her to dance."

"She's our prisoner."

"She's a noblewoman of high birth and a worthy match." He leaned in and spoke in a whisper. "Besides, she's the most beautiful of the maidens here."

Every encounter with her was like an exhilarating challenge. I never knew what to expect, never knew what she might say or do. She was unconventional and bold and determined. Somehow that sparked life inside me in a way I hadn't felt in a long time, if ever. And that scared me.

"If you ask her, I promise I'll stop hounding you," Pitt said. "At least for a few minutes."

"For the rest of the night?"

"For an hour."

"Very well." I pushed away from the table and ignored Pitt's satisfied grin. I'd give him what he wanted and then get an hour of peace. By then, the festivities would likely be nearing their end, and I would be free to retire for the night.

As I approached the women's table, several of the maidens watched me, their anticipation growing. Silently, I berated Pitt for putting me in the position where I would need to break their hearts. I simply wasn't interested in a match no matter how pleasant or pretty they were.

Olivia was actually the perfect choice as a partner for the evening because she wouldn't place expectations upon me for an attachment, not when she was anticipating a union with Lionel Lacy. In fact, even if she didn't have designs on Lionel, she'd never consider me, not when she believed I was nothing more than a lowly knight. Of course, she'd likely taken stock of my wealth. But for a woman like Olivia, wealth would never be enough.

I passed the length of the women's table until I reached the far end. I could sense her attention upon me much the same as the other women. She was interested, or at least curious, in my next choice. That realization bolstered my courage as I halted next to her.

"My lady." I bowed and offered her my hand. "Would you honor me with your company for the next dance?" It was the same question I'd posed to the other women, nothing more and nothing less.

Yet, Olivia's eyes flashed as though mocking me for my unoriginality. "Since you are clearly weary of the proceedings, I shall not tax you further."

I was surprised she'd read me so well. But I attempted to keep any further emotions from showing. "I'm not too weary to dance with you."

"And what if I am too weary to dance with you?" She toyed with the stem of her goblet, turning it around. Next to her, Isabelle watched our exchange, her blue eyes wide with trepidation, likely worried what Olivia might say or do next.

From the lift of Olivia's chin and set of her mouth, I sensed she had no intention of dancing with me, especially if she believed I was only asking her out of obligation and had no desire to be with her. She was a proud and stubborn woman, one who wouldn't be easily swayed, and I had no wish to battle her this eve.

Yet, from the corner of my eye, I could see Pitt watching my interaction with Lady Olivia with almost gleeful interest. He wouldn't be satisfied if I returned to the table without engaging this feisty prisoner of ours in a dance. He might even order me to return and ask her again.

Having now garnered the attention of the other women as well as nearby guests, I would need to persuade Lady Olivia to dance. And there was one way to make her do anything.

I bent so that I was close to her ear. "If you don't accept this dance, you'll force me to ask Lady Isabelle. And I know you don't want me drawing attention to her any more than I do."

My whisper had the desired effect. Olivia stiffened and lifted defiant eyes to me. "You would not dare."

"You might leave me no choice."

She released her goblet and gave me a cold look. "Very well. I shall dance with you. But you should know most women prefer to be enticed onto the dance floor, not forced."

"Do you wish that I entice you, my lady?" I asked, holding out my hand to her again.

"I doubt you could even if you put the whole of your effort into it."

Her declaration issued a silent challenge, one that made my insides quicken. I wanted to prove her wrong, wanted to show her I was capable of wooing and winning any woman I set my sights upon.

She rose from her spot on the bench as regally as if she were a queen, her shoulders squared, her chin high. When she placed her fingers into mine, however, she couldn't hide the tremble, the one that told me I affected her the same way she did me.

I was normally a rigidly self-controlled person and could hold myself aloof in most situations. But this woman caused me to lose all sense of objectivity every time she was near.

One dance, I silently admonished. I'd keep her at arm's length, just as I had with all the other women. Then I'd be done for the night.

I led her to the center of the hall where the tables and benches had been pushed against the walls to make room for the dancing.

"You might be quite inept at wooing a woman," she said, positioning herself in front of me for the dance. "But rest assured, you are quite accomplished at playing the part of a poppet on a stick for Lord Pitt."

"Poppet on a stick?" I couldn't contain my humor. Laughter bubbled up, and I found myself chuckling at her analogy.

Her chin rose a notch higher, tilting her pretty face up to mine. "I have no doubt if Lord Pitt asked you to jump up onto the table and entertain him like a jester, you would."

I laughed again, and the release made me feel lighter. With one hand I took hold of her waist, and with the other directed our hands upward so that they were pointed together. "Pray tell, what else do you think I would do as Lord Pitt's poppet?"

As I began to lead her through the motions of

the dance, she followed. Her footsteps tapped out the rhythm as expertly as mine. She'd been taught to dance just as I had, and the movements required very little thought and allowed us to continue bantering.

"Lord Pitt wants his favorite poppet to find a wife." Her lips curled into a semblance of a smile, one that lit her eyes.

"He only wishes for my happiness."

"And would taking a wife make you happy, sir?"

"Not in the least." She already knew my stance on remarrying. Her questions were only an attempt to goad me, and I wouldn't give her the pleasure of reacting.

"Then am I to assume Lord Pitt is wrong in his assessment of what you need."

"He meddles where he shouldn't."

"So you will deny him what he wants?"

"I give him what he wants by keeping his coffers full and his enemies subdued."

She studied my face. "Does that mean you will defy your master and refuse to take a bride from among these women as he bids you to do?"

"I think you know I am no one's poppet, my lady." My voice came out low, almost a growl. She had to know by now I wasn't a weakling. If she didn't then I would find a way to show her.

Her long lashes swept down and made my stomach do a strange freefall. It was a sensation that made me forget about all the reasons why I shouldn't feel attracted to her. Why did this woman seem to have the power to disarm me by one look, one touch, one bat of her eyelashes? Was I wrong? Was I a poppet after all?

"It is easy to see that Lord Pitt regards you affectionately, more like a father than a master."

"He's not my master." I relished the gentle curve of Olivia's hip beneath my fingers. The sway was graceful and womanly and made me all the more conscious of how lovely she was. "I've chosen to serve him and could release myself from that servitude at any time."

"Then he has awarded you land and a home for your daring deeds?"

"No." I had no need of land or a home. Maidstone was sufficient enough. "You have seen for yourself what Lord Pitt awards me, my lady."

At my reference to her earlier appearance in my chambers, her sights dropped to the pin that fastened my mantle. It was oval and studded with sapphires that matched the rich blue of my garments. The pin had once belonged to my father and the previous Barons of Hampton before him. I rarely wore anything but my simple woolen soldier's hose and tunic. But tonight I'd taken more care with my appearance. With Olivia in such close proximity, I was suddenly glad that I'd worn garments and jewels befitting one of my status.

"Yes, indeed I have seen what Lord Pitt awards you." Her voice dripped with disdain. She released her hold at my waist and reached up to touch the pin.

"That pin belonged to my father and his father before him." I didn't normally feel the need to rise to my defense. But I couldn't allow my father's name to be defamed, especially after my past action had already damaged my family's reputation and fortune.

My father had come from a long bloodline of Norsemen who had once pillaged and raided the land. During those raids, my ancestors had taken an interest in relics, books, and artwork and secretly rescued them from burning monasteries, saving the items from going up in flames with everything else.

Although my great-grandfather had tried to return some of the stolen treasures, many of the old monasteries were gone and those that remained were no longer interested in housing the ancient works. As a result, my family had taken the role of being guardians of the treasures. My father had done so before me. And now it was my duty as baron.

I pressed my hand against the sapphire pin. Underneath my shirt, I felt the outline of the golden chain and the ring it contained. The ring was another treasure my father had given me long ago when he'd entrusted me with Maidstone's treasures.

I was grateful that during the year of drinking

and squandering my family's wealth, I'd revered the relics, books, and artwork enough not to touch them. They'd remained safe as had the ring. Of course, most people wouldn't see value or worth in them the same way my family did. So usually we had no worry of anyone attempting to steal from us.

Nevertheless, if Father had been alive, he would have been sorely disappointed in me. Perhaps that was part of the reason I'd yet to return to Maidstone. Everything there would remind me of my failures.

At least here, very few people knew about the man I'd once been. Everyone respected me, not for my birthright but because of the way I lived and all I'd accomplished.

"You speak with admiration for your father," she remarked after a moment. Her expression and tone had softened as if she'd decided she'd had enough dueling with me for one night. While I rather liked dueling words with her, this softer side reminded me of the conversations we'd had during the long ride to Tolleymuth, the times when she'd let down her guard and we'd talked like friends.

"Will you tell me about him?" she asked.

"My father?"

"Yes." She touched my family heirloom again before caressing the brooch she'd pinned to her bodice. She traced the cross pattern at the center and the emeralds.

"I'll tell you as much about my father as you're willing to share about your mother."

At my suggestion, she smiled with genuine pleasure. The upturn of her lips only made her more beautiful and made me feel suddenly winded, as though I'd been sprinting in one of the battle drills I did with my men every day.

We talked until finally I realized several tunes had come and gone and that I'd danced with her far longer than I had with anyone else.

As I became silent, she did as well. She looked everywhere but me, clearly self-conscious. At the close of the melody, I escorted her back to the women's table, bowed my head, and then turned away, resisting the urge to let myself gaze upon her face again.

I could feel the attention from the other women on my retreat and wondered if she was watching me too. Although I was tempted to look back, I refrained and instead forced myself to walk directly to my seat next to Pitt. With what I hoped was a stoic expression, I lowered myself.

Before my hindquarters hit my chair, Pitt's elbow connected with my ribs. "You're smitten with her."

"She's untamed, undisciplined, and has a sharp tongue." I grabbed my goblet.

"Then she's exactly what you need." Pitt's tone was smug.

Though I wanted to glance at her, I made

myself stare straight ahead. I needed no one. Above all not a woman like Olivia.

"You're a strong man, Windsor," Pitt said, digging his fingers through the bowl of sweet-meats that the servants had delivered to the table during my absence. "You need a strong woman who won't be intimidated or crushed by you."

Had I intimidated Giselle? Was that what I'd done wrong? She'd always been quiet and meek. I'd been surprised when she'd grown increasingly unhappy in our relationship. I hadn't understood what I'd done to push her away and so had only worked harder to keep her close.

In the end, I'd lost her anyway.

I'd failed at being a husband. My mistakes had cost me too much once, and I wouldn't take another chance at failing again.

I gulped down several long sips of my ale then set my goblet down with a resounding clank. "I can't deny that Lady Olivia is a very fine lady. But I have no wish for a bride, strong woman or no."

Pitt sat back in his chair, tossed several honey-covered nuts into his mouth, and then gave me a calculated smile. "Very well, Windsor. If that's your wish, then I'll drop the matter."

"Thank you, my lord." But even as I spoke, I knew I hadn't heard the end of his scheming to find me a wife. For some reason, he believed I wouldn't be whole and happy until I made peace with my past and got married again.

The trouble was, I'd never make peace with my past. And I didn't want to bring any woman, no matter how strong, into the turmoil that haunted me.

Chapter
12

My gown rustled too loudly in the silence, and I fisted the layers to keep them from giving my presence away.

I couldn't believe my fortune. The oaken door to Lord Pitt's solar had been ajar. None of the servants had been in sight. And the inner door to his treasury had been unlocked.

With a glance over my shoulder into the deserted solar, to his empty writing table and chair, to the quiet bedchamber beyond, I assured myself I was alone before I turned my attention to the shelves and the numerous chests on the floor.

Surely the Holy Chalice was in this treasury somewhere.

I held out my candlestick in its ceramic dish, the flame casting a glow over the lowest shelves revealing an assortment of old armor coated with dust and spiderwebs. I lifted the candle-stick to the next shelf noting glass vials of all colors and sizes.

A noise outside the solar—like a banging shutter—brought me to a standstill. I held my breath and listened. My nerves were strung as taut as an embroidery stitch. I had only a few minutes to search before I needed to return to the sewing circle.

I'd pricked my finger with a needle and had asked Lady Glynnis if I might return to my chamber to bandage it. She'd eyed me coldly but also with a glimmer of animosity that had been growing since the dance two nights ago.

The other ladies had been more standoffish as well, regarding me with antagonism that I guessed had something to do with my dance with Sir Aldric. Izzy had commented that the ladies were merely jealous because he'd spent three dances with me and only one with them.

I wanted to tell the other ladies they had nothing to worry about, that since the dance, Aldric had gone out of his way to avoid any encounters with me. He had no designs upon me any more than he did them.

Not that I wanted him to have any designs for me. Yes, I could admit I found him attractive. And yes, I understood why young maidens vied for his attention, especially if the mere sight of him made their pulses quicken as it did mine.

However, he'd been clear he had no intention of marrying again. I could only surmise he'd loved his wife deeply and couldn't fathom loving anyone the same way.

Even if he wasn't in love with his late wife and even if there was something growing between us, I was leaving Tolleymuth soon and would likely never see him again, not after Father finalized my betrothal to Lionel.

The last two nights as I'd lain in bed, I'd tried to picture Lionel and conjure feelings for him. But nothing about him moved me, nothing in his appearance, his speech, or his conduct. I wanted to remember conversations we'd had or smiles we'd shared, but nothing came back to me, except the conversations and smiles I'd shared with Aldric.

"I'll make memories with Lionel," I'd assured myself. "And eventually over time, love will grow between us."

Not all marriages were love matches. Even if my marriage to Lionel never developed into one of love, we would still work together for the greater good of our families. That's what mattered the most—loyalty to family. Feelings would come and go, but family would remain steadfast.

I glanced around the closet, scanning the rest of the shelves, searching for anything that might be worthwhile. So far, the room was turning out to be a storage area for junk rather than treasure.

Stifling a sigh, I dropped in front of one of the chests. I placed the candlestick on the top of another chest before I pulled a pin out of my hair and inserted it into the keyhole. With a few jiggles and jabs, the lock clicked open. Cecil had taught me well.

The chest in Aldric's chamber had been just as easy to open. I still needed to find a way to return to his room so I could finish my search there. And I needed to do it soon. Time was slipping away. Father would be expecting word of my accomplishment any day. He'd placed his faith in me, and I couldn't let him down.

After all, he'd approved of my combat training with Cecil, especially in the days before Charles had been born. In those days, I'd been like a son to him. He'd also allowed, even fostered, my education in languages, mathematics, and the sciences. He'd checked on my progress regularly. And I'd always looked forward to the opportunities to impress him with my knowledge as well as my physical prowess with the sword.

His visits, while infrequent, had been a highlight for me. The rare approval in his eyes had kept me training and learning diligently so I would one day make him truly proud of me.

After Charles's birth, it had taken time for me to notice my father didn't visit me as often at Ludlow, and that when he did, he was no longer interested in my training and education. He took me on fewer hunts and excursions, until eventually he'd stopped altogether.

I'd tried to discover ways to draw his attention back to me. But I'd finally resigned myself to the reality that Charles had replaced me. Father had finally gotten the son he'd longed for, and I'd been relegated to my proper place as a daughter.

When Father began negotiating for my position as the future Marchioness of Clear-water, I'd understood my new role, that I would please Father best and earn his favor again if I made an advantageous match. Such was the place of a daughter. I might not be the center of his attention anymore, but I could still make him proud by the efforts I made in securing a match that would elevate his status and prestige.

Of course, I didn't begrudge Charles Father's affection since he suffered so often from the seizures that left him weak and tired. During the times I'd visited my brother at Wigmore, I witnessed his attacks, his eyes rolling back in his head, his frail frame wracking with uncontrol-lable movements, and his gasping struggles to breathe. I feared for his life every time I watched him go through that. And I lamented his weakness and inability to truly enjoy life.

I understood Father's driving need to find the Holy Chalice. He was seeking a remedy to not only save Charles and lessen his suffering but to improve the quality of his life. Father had been on a mission to find the Holy Chalice for the past year. He'd even gone to the continent in his search.

If he believed Lord Pitt now had the ancient relic, I couldn't fail to find it. Not only did it have the potential to help Charles, but finding it would be one more way I could make my father take notice of me and appreciate my skills. Perhaps he'd love me again, the way he had before Charles had been born.

After another glance over my shoulder to make certain I was still alone, I lifted the lid of the first treasure chest. Silver and gold coins glimmered in the amber candlelight. I wasn't interested in the coins. Instead, I dug my hand through the pile and searched beneath for anything else buried there. The clinking of the metal seemed to echo off the walls, and I was sure the women in the corner of the great hall could hear my searching.

"Check in Lord Pitt's solar," came a woman's voice.

I jerked back, removing my hand from the chest. At my hasty movement, some of the coins slid from the pile and spilled onto the floor with a decisive jangle.

"In there!" The woman's voice was louder, and I recognized it as belonging to Lady Glynnis. "In the treasury closet!"

I lowered the lid of the chest and scrambled away from it while frantically searching for a hiding place. None of the chests were big enough and none wide enough to fit inside.

The rapid footsteps approaching the half-open door told me that not only would I find no place to hide, but I also wouldn't be able to make an escape. My sights returned to the bottom shelf with the dusty armor. Were there any old weapons I could use to fight my way free?

I saw nothing that would be helpful and resigned myself to the only option I had left: stay and make an excuse for why I was in Lord Pitt's treasury room, then pray everyone believed me.

The door swung wide, and the light from the arched windows poured inside revealing me standing in the middle of the treasury room.

A tall knight I recognized from among Aldric's men filled the doorway. Behind him two other knights approached. And a woman wearing an elaborate headdress.

The heavily padded roll with dangling jewels belonged to none other than Lady Glynnis. As she pushed her way forward, the knights stepped aside, allowing her access to the treasury room.

Her hefty chest rose and fell in labored breathing, and her fleshy cheeks were red from exertion.

Had she followed me after I left the sewing circle? If she'd hurried after me, perhaps she'd noticed that I'd veered off into her husband's chambers instead of ascending to the next floor where the women's rooms were located.

"Arrest this woman." Lady Glynnis pointed her bejeweled hand at me, her fingers laden with rings and her wrists with bracelets and ribbons.

"My lady, I was only searching for a vial of medicine to ease the sting of my cut." I swiped up one of the glass bottles from the shelf.

"You're a thief." Her words were sharp and her small dark eyes full of accusation. "Just as I suspected."

"No," I replied hastily. "I assure you. I have no intention of stealing." I'd only planned to take the chalice to heal my brother. That wasn't the same as stealing out of greed, was it?

"Then why did you open the chest?" She glanced at the unlatched lock along with the telltale coins scattered on the floor.

"It was already ajar." Surely God would forgive me for my lie. After all, I was doing this for Charles and my father, not for myself.

"I see you are a thief and a liar," Lady Glynnis retorted. "I suspected as much."

I shook my head but before I could find another excuse, something to extract me from my guilt, she turned to the knights. "Lock her in chains and throw her in the dungeons."

Panic churned inside like a wagon wheel spinning in mud. "No, my lady. You are mistaken."

"The only mistake I've made is not discovering and exposing your thievery to his lordship sooner." She motioned the knights to seize me.

Had she purposefully laid a trap for me? Was that why Lord Pitt's chambers were deserted and the doors unlocked?

I groaned inwardly at my foolishness. I should have known my search was too easy. I should have suspected Lady Glynnis would be looking for a way to punish me for drawing Aldric's attention during the feast away from her favored ladies. Throwing me into a dungeon would ensure I was out of the way—perhaps even permanently if Lord Pitt was angry enough.

I took a step further into the closet. I needed a way to remove myself from the pit I'd dug for myself.

"I demand to see Sir Aldric," I addressed the knights. Aldric had protected me and made certain others treated me with respect and kindness. He would be my ally now—at least I hoped he would. "I insist you take me to your commander."

"He's away, my lady," said the tall knight closest to me.

"It's of no consequence one way or the other," Lady Glynnis said. "There's nothing he can do to help you."

"Should we wait for his return?" the tall knight asked. "She is his prisoner."

Lady Glynnis glared at him. "If you refuse to obey me and lock this thief and imposter away, I shall report you to my husband directly and make sure you are severely punished."

Since coming to live at Tolleymuth, I'd heard enough tales from the other women to know that while Lord Pitt was fair, he was strict with his men and held them to the highest standard. He certainly wouldn't tolerate any form of disrespect, especially to his wife.

As if concluding the same, the knights moved forward, their swords clanking against their chain mail. The tall knight again hesitated before taking hold of my arm. "I'm sorry, my lady."

I considered resisting. Cecil had taught me how to fight with my fists. While I wasn't as proficient with my hands as I was with the sword, I was lithe and nimble compared to these men. I'd likely be able to get away from them.

But where would I go if I escaped? Lady Glynnis would only demand that the knights search the grounds until they found me. Then they'd throw me in the dungeons anyway and perhaps lock Izzy with me.

If I went with them now, I'd prevent Izzy from suffering the same fate. At least I prayed she would remain safe.

The tall knight tugged me forward, and I allowed him to pull me out of the treasury into the solar. "Should we take her to the tower?"

Lady Glynnis shook her head, her eyes now glittering with self-satisfaction. "I told you to take her to the dungeons. She broke into Lord Pitt's treasury and attempted to steal from him. After his kindness and trust, she has betrayed him and deserves to suffer as the prisoner she is."

The knight nodded his acquiescence. One of the others took my opposite arm, wedging me between them while the third knight moved ahead to lead the way.

As they ushered me out of Lord Pitt's chambers, my thoughts whirred in every direction. One clamored louder than the rest: I'd failed to find the Holy Chalice and now likely had lost my chance to finish searching for it. Even if Lord Pitt showed mercy and didn't make me languish in the dungeons, he would no longer allow me to roam around the castle unsupervised. He'd keep me under close surveillance for the duration of my captivity.

A heavy burden fell upon my heart. I'd failed my brother. More than that, I'd failed my father. I dreaded the news I would have to send him, that I hadn't been able to do the one thing he'd specifically sent me to do. I'd hoped to earn more of his love, but now I'd likely lost what little that remained.

I didn't resist the knights as they led me down long hallways and winding stairwells. When the first knight finally unlocked and opened a thick door, the damp waft of cool musty air that greeted me told me we'd reached the dungeons.

After lighting a torch, the knights guided me down many steps that went deep into the earth. The darkness and dankness circled around me, making me shiver and wish I'd brought my cloak.

At the bottom, we turned into a low-ceilinged tunnel made of stone. Along either side were cave-like rooms barred shut with iron grates. As far as I could tell, they were empty of other prisoners.

We stopped in front of the first grated door. The leading knight inserted a key and wrenched the door open, its hinges squealing loudly as if the door hadn't been used in a while.

By the torchlight, I could see the curving walls containing iron rings used to further secure more dangerous criminals. Old hay was strewn in loose piles across the dirt floor, and strands of broken webs hung from the ceiling. Other than a flat pallet, a triple-legged stool, and a tin chamber pot, the cell was devoid of any furnishings.

I walked inside of my own accord and stopped in the center to gather my bearings. The knights closed and locked the grate, and I watched them as if in a dream.

As the knights retreated toward the stairway, the tall one lingered, peering at me with anxious eyes. "Is there anything I can get you, my lady?"

"When Sir Aldric returns, will you take him word of my predicament?"

"He's gone hunting and will be away for several days."

For a moment, I considered the possibility that later I could pick my cell lock with one of my hairpins and make my escape from Lord Pitt. But my situation was far different from when Izzy and I had tried to escape during the ride to Tolleymuth.

Now I was hemmed in on all sides by the thick castle walls. I would have too many obstacles and guards to overcome. By myself, I might be able to accomplish it. But if I attempted such an escape with Izzy, I'd only endanger her further. And I certainly couldn't leave her behind.

For now, I had to bide my time in the dungeons. I expelled a defeated breath but just as quickly lifted my chin. "Then will you see that no harm befalls Lady Isabelle?"

"Very well, my lady." He bowed his head. "I'll do my best."

"Thank you."

He hurried after the other knights, their footsteps pounding the stairs as they ascended, taking the light with them and leaving me in utter blackness. And despair.

Chapter 13

THE BRAYING OF THE HOUNDS WELCOMED OUR HORSES through the gatehouse. The dogs were likely complaining they hadn't been allowed to accompany us, believing like everyone else that we'd gone hunting. Rather, our riding expedition over the past few days had taken us near the border so we could spy on the clandestine dealings the Marcher barons continued to have with the Welsh.

We'd returned with a half a dozen hare and several quail, which weren't nearly enough to account for the length we'd been away. Nevertheless, the game would provide a cover if anyone asked of our whereabouts.

The past few July days had been hot. Grit filled every crevice of my face, and my tongue was parched. I would relish a cool splash and drink from the well.

But even as I nudged my horse into the inner bailey toward the well, the downturned gazes of several of the knights by the barracks set my nerves on edge. If they were avoiding making eye contact, then something was amiss.

Immediately I veered toward the men, studying their faces and attempting to read their expressions. Anxiety and wariness were clearly written there.

"What is it?" I called to the cluster.

Before they could answer, Sir Darien and Sir Robert stepped out of the armory and strode toward me.

"What news have you?" I said as I scanned the castle grounds for any signs of distress. Had they engaged in a skirmish or fended off an attack?

"Welcome back, Sir Aldric." Darien reached to take the reins of my horse. I handed them over and slid from my mount.

"Don't waste time with pleasantries, Darien," I rebuked.

"Three days past, Lady Glynnis caught Lady Olivia stealing from Lord Pitt's treasury and had her locked in the dungeons."

A knot cinched in my gut and pulled taut with both anger and frustration—mainly at myself for not anticipating that something like this might happen. After catching Olivia rummaging in my chamber, I should have known she'd get herself into further trouble, that she wouldn't be happy with just her mother's brooch. I should have forced her to finally tell me what she was searching for.

"That's not all, sir," Darien continued, his young face solemn.

"Go on."

"Lady Glynnis has petitioned Lord Pitt to hang Lady Olivia as a thief. We've heard rumors the execution will take place on the morrow."

If Pitt had agreed to the execution then the charges against Olivia were indeed substantial and credible. Pitt wouldn't move forward otherwise.

Lady or not, he wasn't afraid to administer justice where it was due. Only last year, Pitt had almost burned Sabine at the stake to determine whether she was a witch. Bennet had denied the charges against her. And although I hadn't been sure what the markings on Sabine's arms meant, whether she was truly innocent, I'd fought for her freedom alongside Bennet because he'd loved and believed in her.

If Pitt could threaten Sabine's life, I had no doubt he'd kill Olivia in order to administer justice as well as show his strength and superiority. I understood he couldn't allow a crime like Olivia's to remain unpunished. He had to exact swift justice, or he would only encourage others to question his authority.

I spun and began to stalk toward the keep. I had to convince Pitt not to execute Lady Olivia. Surely he could find some other way to punish her besides taking her life.

My pulse thudded a hard tempo that matched my heavy steps. By the time I entered the dark interior, a quiet desperation had gripped my muscles, making me turn my steps in the direction of the stairwell that would take me to the dungeons.

As I descended with several knights following closely behind, I held up a hand to halt them. "Wait for me here," I said tersely, as I took the torch from the closest guard and resumed my descent.

When I reached the bottom of the long stairway, I held the torch up and scanned the cells for her.

"Lady Olivia," I said softly. "It is I, Sir Aldric."

At my voice, a scuffling in the first cavern drew my attention. I shifted the torch so that its light fell past the grated door. Inside, Lady Olivia rose to a sitting position on a pallet. She blinked, her eyes not accustomed to the light. Her hair had come loose from her usual neat plaits and coils and now fell in disarray over her shoulders hanging almost to her waist.

She hugged her arms to her chest. "Sir Aldric, I have been waiting for your return." Her words came out stilted through chattering teeth.

A quick scan of her cell revealed its barrenness. She had no blanket, not even a cloak to keep her warm. Although the July day was hot, the temperatures down in the bowels of the earth were always cold and damp.

That she was in the dungeons instead of one of the tower rooms made me angry enough. Surely a woman of her stature should have been given the honor of staying in the tower. The accommodations were sparse but would have been brighter and warmer. To find her here in the dark and cold without any comforts turned my stomach. We weren't brutes, and we would treat ladies, even those accused of thievery, with the respect they were due.

In two long strides, I was at the base of the stairs calling up to my men, "I want several blankets and a cloak brought to me at once." I would, in fact, take her to the tower just as soon as I had the chance to speak to Pitt regarding the transfer.

In the meantime, I would provide her with warmth and light.

"Has anyone fed you?" I said returning to the grate and studying her through the darkness.

"Yes," she stammered, her body visibly shaking. "Several of your men have done what they could to alleviate my discomfort."

I could guess which of my men had done so, and I would reward them later. For now, I needed to release her from the dungeons. I stalked back to the stairs. "Bring me the keys to the cells."

"Lady Glynnis has the keys," Sir Darien called down. "She has made it known that she plans to keep them until it's time for Lady Olivia to receive her punishment."

I wanted to curse Lady Glynnis but swallowed my retort. What reason did her ladyship have to get involved? Had Olivia done something to offend her?

"Where are those blankets?" My voice rose to a shout, but I didn't care.

"They are on the way, sir."

"Send a servant to fetch a hot meal and warm ale for the lady."

"Right away, sir."

I returned to the cell to find that Olivia had moved to the grate and stood only a half a dozen paces away. At the proximity, I could see the smudges of dirt on her pale face, the bits of hay and dust that coated her gown, the evidence that she'd attempted to cover herself with the stale straw for warmth. Her body still shook even as she rubbed her hands over her upper arms in a futile effort to elicit heat.

I was tempted to peel off my hauberk and offer her the tunic underneath. But I was layered in dust and sweat and my garments would smell of the sourness of my travels.

"Come here." I beckoned her closer as I placed the torch in the wall mount.

Thankfully she obeyed without her usual questions or resistance. I reached through the bars, took hold of her arms, and began to slide my hands up and down. Even through the layer of sleeve fabric, her body gave off a chill.

If the bars hadn't stood between us, I would have pulled her into my arms and gladly given her my own heat.

"Here are the blankets, sir." Sir Darien's voice echoed down the corridor, and his footsteps slapped the stairs in his haste.

I released Olivia long enough to grab the blankets and when I returned to her cell, I rapidly unfolded the first coarse linen and wrapped it around her. When I finally had her bundled beneath three blankets, I began rubbing her arms again, this time over the wool.

"How is that?" I asked.

"Much better," she said, her voice less wobbly. She was leaning against one side of the bars and I leaned against the other, the cold beams the only thing standing between us. "I am most grateful."

In the quietness of the dungeons, my breathing was heavy and hers was jagged, filling the thin space between us.

"I'm sorry I wasn't here to prevent you from being locked up down here," I whispered.

"I brought this upon myself," she whispered back.

"Then Lady Glynnis's accusations are true?"

"I was in Lord Pitt's treasury," she conceded. "But I was not stealing. At least not at the moment they found me."

"Lord Pitt will find you guilty for simply being in his treasury."

"I suppose that is what Lady Glynnis would like to see happen."

My pulse gave a lurch. If what my men told me was true, then Pitt had already declared Olivia guilty based on Lady Glynnis's testimony, and made plans to execute her.

I released Olivia's arms. "I must go speak with Lord Pitt."

She lifted shaking hands as if she meant to grab hold of me.

Again as before, I reached through the grates. This time, I grasped her hands in mine. Her fingers were frigid. I pulled them through the bars at the same time that I bent and breathed out hot air over her fingers.

For several moments, I bathed her hands in my warm breath, hoping once again to ease her chill. I could feel her beautiful green eyes upon me, watching my every move.

When I finally straightened and started to release her, she squeezed my hands and prevented me from leaving. "I want you to know," she whispered. "You are the kindest man I have ever known."

"I don't deserve such praise, my lady."

"And I do not give praise unless I truly mean it."

I held her hands for a moment longer, suddenly loathe to leave her in the dungeons alone.

However, I couldn't disregard the proper protocol lest I make the situation worse for her.

That's all my concern amounted to, I told myself as I ascended the stairs a few seconds later. I was only acting as any captain would toward a prisoner he'd captured. Since I'd been the one to take her into captivity, she was my responsibility. And she certainly didn't deserve to die like a common criminal.

Surely I could make Pitt see that.

I hurried to the great hall, and the aromas of the evening meal greeted me—thick smoky venison and yeasty rye bread. The scents reminded me I hadn't eaten properly in over three days. I would relish a fine supper, but only if I was able to convince Pitt to spare Olivia's life and move her to the tower.

As I strode to the front where Pitt was playing chess with one of his trusted older friends, Sir Frank, my mind spun with all the ways I could rise to Olivia's defense, any way I could possibly change his mind about executing Olivia.

I was relieved Lady Glynnis and the other women had dispersed from the corner where they sewed, likely retiring to their chambers to ready themselves for the evening meal and activities. I would have a hard enough time pleading Olivia's case without having to contend with Lady Glynnis's accusations.

I halted a dozen paces away from Pitt out of

respect and waited for him to notice and address me. He finished his move, sat back in his chair, and studied the chessboard while his opponent did the same. I had no doubt he knew I was there and was making me wait as a test of my patience. Under normal circumstances, my patience was unmatched. I could endure high levels of agony without complaint.

But with Olivia languishing in the dungeons, I was anxious to see her removed as soon as possible. I shifted so that my sword clanked. When that elicited no response, I coughed into my hand.

"She's a thief," Pitt growled, apparently knowing exactly what I wanted to discuss.

If he wished for no preamble, then I would give him none. And if he had no qualms about discussing this matter in the presence of Sir Frank, then neither did I. "I'm told she took nothing."

"She picked the lock of one of my chests and was digging through it when Lady Glynnis discovered the treachery."

"She's been searching for something since the day she arrived," I replied. "I know not what item she seeks. But I have observed her searching at other times." I decided against revealing I'd caught her in my private chambers. I didn't want to besmear Olivia's reputation any more than it already was.

"Then she is a sneak as well as a thief."

"If she really wanted to fill her family's coffers

by taking from you, then she would have stashed the stolen goods away. But she had nothing in her chambers, as I'm sure you discovered."

"Yes, the guards searched her rooms and found nothing. But that doesn't mean that she didn't hide the stolen goods elsewhere."

"Is anything missing?"

"No."

"Then everything is accounted for?"

Finally, Pitt shifted his attention away from the game board to me. His eyes were dark, making the pale scar running down his face stand out. "She was caught in my treasury up to her arms in one of my chests. I must punish her with a hanging as I do other thieves."

"She's a noblewoman, not a criminal."

Pitt crossed his arms and reclined in his high-backed chair, stretching his legs out in front of him, his expression much too calculated for my liking.

My nerves stretched like limbs on the rack. I couldn't let him go through with his plans to hurt Olivia. She didn't deserve it. No woman did.

"If you hang her, you'll start a war," I warned. "Her father will gather his allies and attack Tolleymuth."

"Then we'll fight and destroy them."

"In so doing, you'll risk harming the king's efforts to bring the Marcher barons into submission."

Sir Frank spoke for the first time. "Sir Aldric is right. You would cause a war."

I nodded my thanks to the older man. We all knew the king didn't want to start a war if we could bring about peace some other way.

Pitt steepled his hands beneath his chin and regarded me through narrowed eyes. "If not hanging, then what punishment shall I give the earl's daughter?"

"Move her to the tower and keep her locked there."

"And . . ."

My mind returned to the idea that had fostered at the tournament. If we threatened her match with Lionel Lacy, we would alarm her father and draw him to Tolleymuth. "We can threaten the earl's alliance with Marquess of Clearwater."

Pitt didn't respond but watched me intently as though waiting for me to continue with my plan. I took heart that he was considering other options for Olivia.

"As you know, the earl is in the process of betrothing Lady Olivia to the marquess's son. Such a union will increase the earl's power among the Marcher barons. If we interfere with her betrothal to the marquess's son, her father will finally come and pay her ransom. He wouldn't risk losing such a prestigious match."

"And how is that punishment for her?"

"She's loyal to her father and won't want to

lose the match either. Besides, she's proud. If you give her to a landless knight without status, she'll be appalled and humiliated. I can think of several of my knights who might agree to the plan." Perhaps I could persuade Darien or one of my other faithful knights to do the deed, more so if they knew Olivia's father wouldn't allow her to go through with the marriage. Or at least I hoped her father wouldn't allow it.

"So you're suggesting I shame her?"

"Yes. Such a betrothal would be beneath her, and she'd loathe it." While I didn't want to expose Olivia to any shame, she must suffer or Pitt wouldn't consider the punishment sufficient.

Pitt studied me with the same calculation that again set my nerves on edge. "I expected that once you discovered her life was in danger, you'd offer to marry her in order to save her."

He'd expected me to marry her? I shook my head. "No, my lord." My mind scrambled for an excuse. "I couldn't possibly—"

"I took you for a jealous man, Windsor. I've noticed the way you regard her, and I didn't think you could hand her over to another so easily."

"I'm not jealous, my lord. Besides, the betrothal won't last."

"And if the earl chooses not to ransom his daughter, then you won't mind one of the other knights marrying Lady Olivia?"

My mind flashed with the image of Darien

bending in to kiss Olivia's pretty lips. The mere thought of it sent a sharp, almost violent streak of protest through my blood.

Pitt was gauging my reaction. With a satisfied smile, he sat forward and moved a knight on the chessboard. "I shall grant your request, Windsor, and shall stay Lady Olivia's execution. But only if you agree to the betrothal for yourself."

I couldn't speak past my frustration. Had I played right into Pitt's ploy? Had he planned to entrap me all along?

When he'd told me he would drop the matter of my taking a bride, I should have realized he wouldn't cease his scheming, should have known he was too cunning. But why not force my hand with one of the other women? Why Olivia?

"Surely you don't want me to unite with our enemy?" I offered.

"Keeping the enemy close is oft a wise strategy."

"Very true," remarked Sir Frank as he lifted his pawn and moved it within striking distance to Pitt's queen.

Pitt was quiet as he studied the board.

"At the very least," I said, "allow me to move Lady Olivia to a tower room." I couldn't bear the prospect of her languishing in the dungeons, shaking and cold and hungry any longer than necessary.

"I shall allow the move only after an official

betrothal ceremony." His voice contained a finality that told me he wouldn't be persuaded otherwise.

I stifled an exasperated sigh. "Then I shall make the arrangements for the ceremony right away."

"Good."

Good? I quelled my irritation, certain now Pitt had meddled and had me in the exact position he'd wanted.

"You needn't worry," Pitt said as if sensing my irritation. "You said yourself the betrothal won't last."

"And if it does?"

"Then you may find yourself deliriously happy again, my friend." When he looked at me this time, his eyes brimmed with sincerity. And I realized he thought he was doing this for my good. He believed I cared about Olivia and that somehow she'd make me happy.

Although I wasn't pleased with his stipulations, I knew he meant well. And I couldn't fault him for that. Even if he was wrong.

Chapter
14

Izzy hugged me as though she never meant to let go.

I returned the embrace wholeheartedly, relieved for the opportunity to be with her again—an opportunity I thought I'd lost forevermore.

Sir Darien waited nearby looking discreetly away, allowing me the opportunity to be with my sister.

We stood at the top of the dungeons' stairwell in a deserted hallway. Wrapped in the blankets Aldric had provided for me, my limbs were regaining warmth. Though the castle passageway was drafty, it was warmer than my cell and reflected the heat of summer.

Determined, purposeful steps drew nearer. Aldric's steps.

I suspected he was behind my release. But

what was to become of me now? I had no desire to return to the cold hovel where, save for the rats and spiders, I was alone. Not only had the cold seeped into my very bones, so had fear. I'd never considered myself an easily frightened woman, had always believed myself to be strong natured. But my imagination had too much time to spin tales and had run away with every possible outcome and punishment.

I'd prayed as I never had before. During the prayers, I sensed God's displeasure for how I'd conducted myself. I'd justified my lying and plans to steal because of my desire to help Charles and please my father. I'd told myself what I was doing couldn't be wrong if I was doing it for the right reasons, especially because I believed taking the chalice wouldn't hurt Lord Pitt. After all, he had so many treasures and wouldn't miss one little thing.

But the more I contemplated my actions, I couldn't help but wonder what would happen if the whole of civilization lived by my principle. Where would the wrongdoing stop if everyone acted out whatever moral code felt right in the moment?

If I felt I could justify stealing, then someone else might justify killing or lying or cheating. Where would the justifying stop? After all, a person's heart could often be deceptive and greedy, lulling them into doing something that might feel right in the moment, but ultimately was driven by mixed motives.

As altruistic as I believed my motives were in finding the Holy Chalice, underneath the desire to help my brother and family, I was also doing it for selfish reasons. I wanted to be my father's favorite child. I wanted his approval and love so that I could feel better about myself.

All this time, I'd told myself I was being a loyal daughter. But maybe I didn't really know what true loyalty entailed.

Whatever the case, I was grateful to be aboveground. But I wasn't naïve enough to think that I was being freed, nor was I fool enough to believe my punishment would be suspended. In fact, I'd come to the conclusion I deserved to be disciplined for what I'd done. I just hoped Aldric could convince Lord Pitt to spare Izzy any trouble. This was my fault, not hers.

I gave Izzy a final squeeze and kissed her cheek before I pulled back. She quickly swiped at the tears that had escaped and gave me a wobbly smile. Her fear was like a living force. Even at fifteen, she still relied upon me to be the strong one, to direct her, and to smooth over any problems. What would she do without me to keep her safe? As much as I hated to admit it, I knew deep inside that Father wouldn't bother with Izzy. He never had. And he'd only do so if it served his purposes.

Aldric's admonition regarding my father taunted me: *He seeks to increase his wealth and power in whatever way suits him.*

Was Father doing the same thing to me? Was he using me to serve his purposes regardless of my well-being?

I shook my head. I had to believe he'd heard about my imprisonment and that he was finally making plans to rescue Izzy and me. He might not be able to save me from my crime, but at least he could ransom Izzy. Even as I tried to assure myself of his care, doubts assailed me.

"I see Lady Glynnis cooperated," Aldric said to Sir Darien.

The young knight grinned. "She wasn't happy to relinquish the keys, but she dared not disobey Lord Pitt."

I clutched the blankets over my filthy garments as I faced Aldric. Now that I could see him more completely outside of the darkness of the dungeons, my stomach fluttered with the awareness of just how attractive he was with his rugged and battle-hardened features. His chiseled jaw was covered in several day's worth of stubble, the creases in his forehead lined with dust.

My thoughts returned to the intimate moment in the dungeons when he'd rubbed my arms to warm me. The friction had helped ease my discomfort, but more than that, his touch had ignited sparks inside me. And when he'd blown onto my fingers, the sparks had fanned into flames that still burned low.

His dark eyes swept over me, and I was suddenly self-conscious. I wished I'd had the opportunity to change into fresh clothing as well as wash myself and have one of the servants style my hair.

"My lady." He bowed his head toward me but didn't meet my gaze. "We don't have much time, but I've ordered the servants to prepare you a bath and change of gowns."

"Then I do not have to return to the dungeons?"

"No." He glanced at Sir Darien as though he wished the young man would explain my punishment so he didn't have to. But Sir Darien fixed his attention on the floor, his eyes wide with obvious embarrassment.

"You may be honest and tell me my fate," I said, reaching for Izzy's hand and grasping it hard to control the trembling.

"Lady Glynnis petitioned for your execution by hanging . . ."

At his declaration, my knees nearly gave out. I would have fallen if Izzy hadn't slipped her arm around my waist and held me up. Perhaps I should have attempted to escape while I still had the chance, even if it had meant leaving

Izzy behind.

"Have no fear," Aldric said quickly as though sensing my despair. "After I spoke with Lord Pitt, he agreed to stay your execution. You'll be punished instead by betrothal to one of his knights."

Betrothal to one of his knights? For a moment, I could only stare at Aldric in disbelief. Then as Lord Pitt's plan began to sink in and make sense, I shuddered. He was cutting off the possibility of my family's alliance with the Marquess of Clearwater in order to anger my father further.

But would the move make any difference? After my father's absence thus far, I could no longer predict what he might do next. Perhaps he'd lost interest in an alliance with the marquess. Perhaps he no longer saw me as an asset and would let Lord Pitt do what he wished with me.

Whatever the case, I was thankful Lord Pitt would allow me to live. And I was thankful to Aldric for rescuing me from the dungeons and death. "I deserve the punishment. And I understand the intent to draw out my father and make him finally pay the ransom."

"It was the best I could do for you, my lady." His voice and eyes contained an apology.

I understood then what he'd left unsaid, that if my father still refused to pay the ransom money and remained unwilling to subject himself to Lord Pitt and thereby the king, then I would be obligated to marry the knight underneath my rank and quite possibly live in poverty and obscurity. Such a sentence was indeed serious punishment for a noblewoman like myself, especially after I'd already envisioned myself living at court as an attendant to the queen.

I straightened and lifted my shoulders in an attempt to be brave. At least I would be alive and would have more time to figure a way out of my predicament. "Again, I thank you for using your influence to save me. You were more than generous to avail yourself of my plight."

"You wouldn't be in this plight if I hadn't taken you from your home."

"I cannot fault you for what your master ordered you to do."

Our gazes connected in a moment of understanding. In some ways, we were both pawns in a game much larger than ourselves.

"The betrothal ceremony is to take place at once," he said. "Afterward Lord Pitt will allow me to move you to the tower. It won't be as comfortable as your previous guest chamber, but it'll be much better than the dungeons."

"I shall not complain."

"Then we need to be on our way and finalize the betrothal before Lady Glynnis persuades

Lord Pitt to change his mind."

"Very well, sir. I shall make haste."

"The ceremony will be in the chapel," Aldric said to Sir Darien. "Have the ladies there at the next ring of the bells."

Sir Darien nodded.

Aldric spun and began to stalk away. As I watched him, I realized I'd neglected to ask about the knight chosen for my betrothal, likely the lowliest and poorest among the ranks. Was it someone I already knew? Hopefully one of Aldric's loyal men. At least they'd been kind to me.

"Who am I to pledge myself to?"

Aldric's footsteps faltered only slightly. Without turning, he spoke over his shoulder. "Me."

The one word rendered me speechless, and I could only watch as he rounded the corner and disappeared from sight.

A distant bell rang the call to Vespers as Sir Darien stopped in front of the open chapel door.

Izzy fidgeted with the caul of gold thread that encased my hair like a net. A jeweled coronet held the silk cap in place. Studded with emeralds and pearls, the workmanship was stunning and matched the dark evergreen gown I wore. The gown was lush and trimmed with tiny seed pearls sewn into elaborate embroidered leaves. It was the most beautiful gown I'd ever worn. One of the servants had disclosed that Aldric had handpicked it for the betrothal ceremony.

In preparing for the occasion, he'd given me every luxury I could want—hot bath water, scented oils, perfumed soaps, along with a half a dozen servants to assist my every move. Although I would have relished the chance to soak in the bath until the water cooled, the servants rushed me along so that now I was perfectly cleaned and groomed.

With every passing moment, my guilt had swelled until now it pressed hard in my chest. Aldric had made his wishes known to me on more than one occasion. He had no interest in taking another wife. In fact, he'd been quite adamant that he planned to remain single.

I had the feeling he hadn't changed his mind, that he had no wish to bind himself to me any more than I did to him. But somehow in attempting to save my life, Lord Pitt had cajoled him into this new plan to lure my father into submission. Aldric wouldn't have agreed to the arrangement if he'd had another option.

He was even nobler than I'd realized. Not many men would sacrifice their own desires and plans to save a lady like me from death.

"Are you ready, my lady?" Sir Darien paused in the chapel doorway.

"No, but I have no other choice, do I?"

My guilt pulsed against my rib cage. How could I make Aldric go through with a betrothal? Even though the contract wouldn't be as binding as marriage, it was still a serious move. If I had any hope of getting out of it, Father would have to pay Aldric for a release.

I'd have to start praying Father would be willing to hand over the required amount so Aldric could be free again. In the meantime, I had to go through with the ceremony or face death.

Sir Darien stepped aside to allow me entrance to the chapel. The hum of voices ceased and silence descended. At the front of the small chapel, the priest stood speaking with Aldric and Lord Pitt. Several other of Aldric's closest knights stood a short distance away.

Lady Glynnis sat stiffly on the front padded bench with one of her ladies by her side. While all other heads turned in my direction, she kept her focus unswervingly on the ornate iron cross that hung on the wall behind the altar. I couldn't see her expression, but the stiff hold of her shoulders told me she resented being present and had no wish to act as a witness to the betrothal.

If only she knew how well I understood her resentment. I didn't want to go through with the betrothal any more than she wanted me to.

As I started down the aisle toward the front, I avoided making eye contact with any of the men, including Aldric. I wasn't sure I would be able to state the betrothal vows if I witnessed the pain it was causing him.

When I reached the front, I took my place next to Aldric. I noticed he, too, had taken the time to bathe and groom. Gone was the dust of travel. He'd donned a fancy tunic hemmed with a golden braid. His hair was freshly washed, neatly slicked back into submission, and tied in place. He'd even taken the time to shave so that his face, though still ruggedly handsome, was less foreboding.

He didn't say anything as he offered me the crook of his elbow.

I took it, leaning in as I did so. "I am sorry."

He gave the barest of nods to acknowledge my apology. His jaw was granite, his brows furrowed, and his lips pursed tightly. His attention was upon the priest and didn't swerve.

I had the overwhelming urge to turn around and run from the chapel. But the thought of hanging from a noose and leaving Izzy alone in this world held me in place. I looked at the priest so he'd know I was ready to begin—at least as ready as I could be given the circumstances. With Izzy at my left and Lord Pitt next to Aldric, we had more than enough witnesses. There was nothing stopping us from the betrothal, except that neither of us wanted it.

I vowed silently that I would eventually find a way to release Aldric from his commitment to me even if I had to pay the price myself.

The ceremony was over within minutes, nothing more than simple vows of intent from each of us. When Aldric reached for my hand and touched a ring to my finger, I couldn't mask my surprise. I wanted to tell him he needn't give me anything, that I would find a way to end our betrothal as soon as possible. But as he gently slid the ring down the length of my finger, I shivered with a strange anticipation.

The thick silver band contained a cross at its center and was engraved with a fancy swirl of jewels. It was as lovely as everything else he'd given me today. Was the ring special to him or merely one of the many treasures he'd claimed during his battles against rebel lords?

"Now that you've pledged your troth," Lord Pitt said, clamping Aldric on the shoulder, "you must seal your vows with a kiss."

"We most certainly will not," I started indignantly. But at the rapid warning look Aldric slanted at me, I let my protest die. I guessed, even without him having to explain, that Lord Pitt would take perverse delight in making me do something I had no wish to do, that the only way to stop him from making matters worse was to give him what he wanted.

Yet, I had no desire to kiss Aldric. He might be handsome and chivalrous, but if we had any chance of severing our oaths at some point in the future, we would fare better if we didn't entangle ourselves deeper into the betrothal.

"Do it, Windsor," Lord Pitt cajoled good-naturedly. "I know you've wanted to kiss her since the night of the dance."

I expected Aldric to deny Lord Pitt and to come up with an excuse that would save us both embarrassment. However, he pivoted and at the same time reached for me, fitting one hand on my waist and sliding the other to the small of my back.

As he drew me closer, I couldn't stop my involuntary gasp at his brazenness. But with his eyes fixed upon my mouth, he swooped in and captured my gasp before it could find full expression. His lips powerfully covered mine and moved in a kiss that gave me no option but to respond.

I was innocent in the ways of men and kissing and intimacy. I'd never been kissed, except for the perfunctory pecks on my hands by suitors. Therefore, nothing prepared me for the power of the connection. I could only close my eyes, completely undone.

The kiss had hardly begun when he broke away, almost abruptly. He straightened and released his hold. "There, my lord." He tossed Lord Pitt a grin—one that seemed genuine. "Are you satisfied?"

Lord Pitt grinned in return, his eyes mischievous. "For now."

When Aldric held out his arm to me, I wanted to pull a veil over my face so that I could hide how much I'd enjoyed his kiss— much more than I wanted to admit to myself, much less to him. As I took hold of him, his gaze raked across my face and landed upon my lips. Something smoldered in his eyes, something that stoked the low flames inside me.

Had he been as affected by the kiss as I was? Likely not. After all, he'd once been married and was no novice when it came to showing affection.

I couldn't make more out of the moment than he'd intended. After all, it was just one little kiss. Hopefully one we'd both soon forget.

Chapter 15

ALL I COULD THINK ABOUT WAS KISSING OLIVIA AGAIN. Through every course of the feast, the kiss I'd given her in the chapel replayed in my mind, especially whenever I happened to glance at her mouth—which I tried not to do but seemed unable to avoid, as she was seated beside me.

Every time I turned to converse with her, every time she spoke to one of the other guests at our table, or every time she sipped from her goblet, I was keenly aware of her lips.

Pitt had likely orchestrated the kiss, knowing once I'd tasted of her, I'd want to have more. However, I couldn't give in to the pressure or the pleasure of claiming another kiss. One kiss was already too many.

Perhaps Pitt had anticipated my reaction to Olivia. But I certainly hadn't expected this. Of course, I could acknowledge how beautiful she was in the velvety green gown that made her look like a queen. But I hadn't thought that bending in and giving her a kiss would stir such longing inside me. I suppose I hadn't counted on her responding with such fervor.

In fact, as much as I'd loved Giselle, I could see now that our relationship had been mostly one-sided. I'd adored her, but she hadn't returned my love as ardently.

Not that I loved Olivia or that she loved me. But I had to admit I felt some kind of affection for her. And from the way that she'd responded to my kiss, I could only surmise she harbored feelings for me as well.

I wasn't displeased by the idea that she liked me. If her father refused to come for her, then she wouldn't be entirely unhappy if we had to wed.

"What say you, Windsor?" Pitt asked boisterously from where he sat several seats down. "Shall we have your wedding in one week?"

One week was much too soon. But I ran my thumb pad around the rim of my goblet, needing to take my time in answering Pitt so that my voice remained neutral and noncommittal. If he detected any hesitancy, he would capitalize on it.

Next to me, Olivia shifted uneasily. She was much less adept at hiding her true feelings, which worked to my advantage most of the time. "We must wait two weeks," she hissed. "My father will surely come once he hears of our betrothal." Her eyes flashed with a desperation that pierced me harder than it should have.

What was wrong with me? Her desperation was to be expected. The betrothal wasn't supposed to be pleasant. It was a punishment for her crime.

"You cannot be seriously considering one week," she whispered.

Again, her words lanced through me. Had I already allowed myself to care about her too much? Deep down, had I wanted her to accept our union? Whatever the case, the sting of her rejection hurt more than I expected.

"What will it be?" Pitt asked again.

"One," I retorted loudly and obstinately. I met Olivia's gaze head-on and watched her eyes fill with surprise. Before she could contradict me, I bent in, captured her lips against mine, and kissed her again.

Her hand shot out as though she meant to push me away. But as I pressed our kiss deeper, her fingers clutched at my tunic, fisting the front into a wad, and she returned the kiss as she had earlier with a force that matched mine and left me shaken.

From a distance, I heard Pitt's pleased laughter along with the guffaws of some of the other men.

Before I lost all sense of reason and rationale, I forced myself to pull back and break the kiss.

She ducked her head but not before I caught

sight of the yearning in her eyes.

I let my shoulders relax with the knowledge that whatever she might say, however she might protest, she was drawn to me. I hadn't imagined her fondness, and I wasn't the only one feeling something.

Perhaps I was a fool to agree to Pitt's plans to have the wedding in one week. It would take time for the earl to receive news of the betrothal. Then he would have to travel to Tolleymuth.

But another part of me was afraid that even a week was too long and that I'd lose Olivia either way—whether after one week or two. I had to silently rebuke myself with the reminder that she wasn't really mine, that I couldn't get involved with her, that she'd be better off without me.

I was thankful Lady Glynnis had taken leave of the feasting early, complaining of stomach pains. Only a few of her ladies remained to return to her with tales of my behavior with Olivia, of the kiss and the plans to wed at week's end. She'd taken a disliking to Olivia and wouldn't be pleased with the news. But I suspected she wouldn't attempt to harm Olivia again, not as long as I was at Tolleymuth.

For once, I wasn't ready for the feast to end. I wanted to lounge at the table with Olivia by my side. But exhaustion was evident in every line of her face. The past few days in the dungeons had taken their toll upon her.

I excused myself to escort her to the tower and her new chamber there. Two of my squires accompanied us. As we started up the winding tower steps, I led the way. The further I climbed, the more she lagged behind.

I retraced my steps. "You're tired, my lady."

She nodded. "Yes, I am indeed weary."

I handed my torch to one of the squires. Then without asking permission, I scooped Olivia up into my arms and began to ascend again.

Her eyes widened but she didn't attempt to escape my hold. "You cannot mean to carry me the rest of the way."

"And why not?"

"You are equally tired from your travels."

I was drained from the past few days of riding hard and sleeping little. But I was not so worn-out that I couldn't assist her.

She settled against my chest. "I hope you know I am sorry."

"Have no care," I reassured her. She was lightweight compared with other things I was forced to lift. "You aren't a burden."

"No, I would apologize for our betrothal." Her warm breath tickled my neck. "In spite of your wishes not to remarry, you agreed to Pitt's stipulations in order to save my life."

"As I told you before, I hold myself responsible for bringing you here and putting you at risk."

"But if I had behaved above reproach, like Izzy. . ."

"Izzy is indeed more docile." I had the feeling that docile or not, Olivia's presence at Tolleymuth would have stirred trouble. She was too striking and vibrant to blend in with the other women. She was one of a kind, with a sharp mind and a strong will.

"Since you have been so noble in rescuing me from a perilous fate," she continued, "I had hoped to find a way to grant you your freedom. Two weeks would give me more time."

Was that why she'd wanted to wait two weeks for our wedding? Because she didn't want to impose on me? "And what if I said I didn't want my freedom from you, my lady? What then?"

"But you do," she said. "You were quite adamant at the dance that you had no wish to take a bride. In fact, you indicated that doing so would bring you no joy, only displeasure."

She was right. I had spoken forthrightly about my intentions to avoid Pitt's scheming, that I'd no desire to remarry, that a woman wouldn't make me happy. I still believed that to be true, didn't I?

My steps slowed as I pondered my feelings of late. "I have no doubt the right woman would bring me a great deal of pleasure." My words were much too bold, but I sensed we needed to speak the truth to survive the realities of our situation. And the truth was, I enjoyed Olivia's companionship. "But I wouldn't be able to bring joy to her in return, rather only heartache and disappointment."

"Are you sure you are incapable of bringing a woman joy?" she asked softly. "You have brought much comfort and happiness to me this day with your kindness."

Her gentle words commanded my attention. I dropped my gaze to hers to find genuine appreciation in her eyes. And something more: a beckoning.

Was she asking me to give marriage and love a chance?

I quickly glanced away. Surely I was reading into her expression more than she intended.

We reached the top of the stairwell, and I stepped aside at the thickly paneled door that marked the entrance to the tower room to allow my squires to unlock, enter the room, and light the wall sconces. Once inside, I could see that the servants had obeyed my orders to make the room as comfortable as possible.

The bed, though narrow, was blanketed in a clean coverlet. The mattress was full, the sign that the servants had stuffed it with fresh goose feathers. A small writing table, containing parchment, a quill, an inkpot, along with several books, had been placed under the high barred window. The shutters had been thrown back to allow the night air to cool the room.

The servants had placed Olivia's chest of clothing and other personal items against the opposite wall. They'd followed my instructions and had recovered more of the gowns we'd confiscated from her home and had folded them carefully and laid them on the top of the chest.

I strode across the room and lowered Olivia to the bed. As I released her, I realized suddenly that I had no desire to relinquish my hold. I liked having her close.

Even so, I wrenched my arms away from her, thankful for the presence of the squires waiting outside the door to hold me accountable for my actions. As tempting as it was to linger in Olivia's room and perhaps steal another kiss from her, I needed to proceed with care.

She snuggled into the mattress and released a contented breath at the same time that her lashes fell to her cheeks.

She lay there, still attired in the headdress and gown I'd chosen for her to wear to the betrothal ceremony, and I could only guess how constricting the items were. But she'd been exquisitely beautiful in them, and she'd been pleased to wear something fine and pretty again.

You have brought much comfort and happiness to me this day with your kindness. Her words rippled through me.

Had I really brought her comfort and happiness today?

I'd failed so miserably to bring Giselle happiness. I'd tried to love her, but I'd fallen short. I didn't want that to happen again. But what if it did? What if I somehow failed Olivia too?

I took a step away from the bed, away from the temptation she posed.

She didn't stir. The deep rise and fall of her chest told me she was already asleep.

For a moment, I couldn't move. I could only watch the tawny firelight flicker in waves across her smooth features, highlighting the elegant lines and slopes in her face.

There was the very real possibility I would marry this woman within the week. And while my stomach flipped and floundered at the possibility, it also seemed to tangle itself into knots with every flip.

Could I give myself permission to attempt to love again and hope to get it right this time? Or should I keep my heart closed off? If I kept the barriers up, I would protect Olivia from getting hurt if I failed her.

The last thing I wanted to do was harm her. But a fear deep inside my bones warned that I'd hurt her no matter which way I chose.

Chapter 16

"What are we doing today?" I asked Aldric as he led me down the spiraling tower stairs.

"You must wait and see, my lady," he answered patiently. Thankfully, in addition to patience, his voice hinted at humor.

For the past three days, he'd come to my high prison tower every late afternoon. Apparently, Pitt had granted him permission to allow me the reprieve from my confinement only if I remained with him for the duration of the outings.

The first day we'd strolled among the castle gardens. I'd basked in every moment of the sunshine and fresh air, reluctant to return to my room when the time together came to a close.

The next afternoon, because of the rain, we'd walked the long passageways of the castle, and had eventually raced up and down opposite stairwells to see who was the fastest. While Aldric had won almost every contest, we'd laughed breathlessly together after each challenge.

Yesterday had been dismal and rainy again. I'd been delighted when he'd ushered me into a large room in the barracks where we'd practiced sword drills. Although we'd used nothing more than blunt wooden training swords, I'd appreciated the chance to practice my skills. And I'd also enjoyed surprising him and his squires with my abilities.

Today had dawned with brilliant sunshine. I hoped we would be able to spend our time together outside again. Although truthfully, I'd decided it didn't matter what we did or where we went. His companionship was enough. He was easy to talk to, enjoyable to be with, and challenged me to be better—to be kinder, nobler, wiser—like him.

"I was afraid I would go mad with the waiting today," I admitted.

Rather than chain mail, he was attired in a silver-blue gipon that fell to his knees. The vest-like garment worn over his shirt buttoned up the front with elegantly embroidered silver buttonholes. The hue made his midnight eyes a shade lighter so that they were a riveting blue.

With his fine garments, along with his dark hair tied back with the leather strap and his face freshly shaven, he was less warrior today and more nobleman. Either way, I always seemed to find myself overly enamored, and I worked hard to temper my desire to stare at him.

"I'm told Izzy spent the greater part of the day with you," he replied over his shoulder.

"Yes." I sighed, stepping out of the tower into the long connecting hallway where his squires waited in the arched doorway that led outside. "I enjoy her company. I really do. But our interests are so diverse, and we have little in common."

"Are you admitting you have a better time with me than Izzy?"

"I shall admit to no such thing," I teased, "unless you take me boar hunting with you on the morrow." He'd already warned me he would be gone all day with the hunt and that I wouldn't see him until much later upon his return. I'd pestered him to take me along, but he'd only shaken his head in refusal.

"It's too dangerous," he declared.

"You have witnessed my skill," I retorted. "You know I am unsurpassed."

He only chuckled before giving me his usual excuse: "Boars are wild and unpredictable."

"But I have you to keep me safe." With him, I was completely protected. He'd rescued me from the dungeons and death. What could befall me now that was any worse?

"That's because you have witnessed my skill," he said in mock solemnity, "and know I'm unsurpassed."

It was my turn to laugh. "Is there nothing I can do to persuade you to take me with you?"

He turned, cocked his head, and watched me for a minute as though contemplating my question, which I knew he wasn't.

Nevertheless, I loved his eyes, the rich dark blue that at times could be penetrating and intense but at other times were light and playful. The slanted angle of his brows only served to draw me in further so that I was liable to drown in his eyes if he looked at me long enough.

Even though an invisible force seemed to pull us together—or at least pull me toward him—he somehow managed to maintain a proper distance during our outings. Of course, having his squires as our constant chaperones helped to keep our interactions platonic so that we'd had no opportunities to repeat the kisses we'd exchanged on our betrothal day.

I could readily admit I wanted him to kiss me again. I'd relived the two he'd given me a dozen times. And every time I did, warm pleasure whispered through me.

"Well?" I queried, my voice echoing in the empty stone passageway. "Is there nothing, then, that I may do to change your mind about the hunt?"

"There may be one thing," he said. "But I don't think you'll like it."

"What is it?"

He glanced toward his squires, still waiting for us near the doorway, and then lowered his voice. "Lord Pitt insists I have treated you like one of my knights rather than my betrothed."

Only three days remained until our wedding, but neither of us brought up the looming deadline. In fact, we didn't talk about the betrothal either, as if by ignoring it we could somehow forget it had happened.

But as the deadline approached, so did the conflict we'd attempted to hold at arm's length. For all his kisses and his bluster about not wanting his freedom, he was only marrying me out of obligation. And for all my infatuation with him, I wasn't sure I was ready to give up so easily on my father. If I willingly married Aldric, I'd forfeit my loyalty to my family. Since I'd always put my family's needs above my own and had done everything my father asked, I wasn't sure I could—or even wanted to—make the change.

"If you treat me like one of your knights, why should Lord Pitt care?" I asked, the lightness I'd felt a moment ago falling away.

Aldric studied my face carefully, and I suspected he could read my every feeling and thought. "Lord Pitt believes I need to woo you more than I have."

I wanted to ask why that would make any difference. Lord Pitt had given me little choice but to marry Aldric whether he wooed me or not. "I do not wish to be wooed."

"I predicted as much."

"I do appreciate your kind gestures," I replied, not wishing him to think I was ungrateful. "But what difference will wooing make when I must marry you or face the hangman's noose?"

Aldric's eyes took on the haunted quality that told me he was troubled in spirit, likely thinking of the mistakes he believed were unforgivable. Was Lord Pitt orchestrating our betrothal and wedding more for Aldric than for me? Perhaps the older man, out of his fatherly affection for Aldric, was trying to help his commander recover from his past pains. Perhaps he believed if Aldric married again, the knight might finally be able to bury his grief over his previous wife.

It was a clever plot, one Aldric had tried to avoid, and likely would have continued to avoid if I hadn't gotten caught in Lord Pitt's treasury. Now that Aldric was trapped into our betrothal, Lord Pitt was still meddling and pushing Aldric to develop his feelings for me.

I wanted to sigh in frustration. "How does

Lord Pitt wish you to woo me?"

"I am to plan a special outing."

"An outing?"

He nodded, refusing to meet my gaze this time, which told me he was embarrassed.

"And if we both willingly subject ourselves to such an outing, will he allow me to accompany you on the boar hunt on the morrow?"

"As long as you ride with me, on my horse. Lord Pitt insists that if I take you outside castle walls, you are to be with me at all times."

I rolled my eyes in an unladylike fashion and almost smiled at Lord Pitt's pathetic attempts at matchmaking. "Very well, sir. I shall go on any outing you wish. And I shall ride with you on your steed for the hunt."

His eyes widened just slightly. "I hadn't expected such easy acquiescence, my lady."

"Ever since you regaled me with your boar hunting escapades, I have been hoping for the opportunity to go. Thus I cannot neglect the adventure when it is within my grasp."

His lips curled into the beginning of a smile. "Very well. Then let us be on our way to the outing."

It was my turn to be surprised. "I thought you needed to plan it."

"I have."

"You planned an outing even though you knew not whether I would agree to it?"

His brows rose giving light to his eyes. "I took a chance."

"And what would you have done had I not acquiesced so easily?"

"Persuaded you." His voice dropped low. His gaze dropped as well, landing upon my lips and revealing how he'd planned to persuade me.

My pulse began to thrum. Had he resigned himself to our impending marriage? Was he finally ready to lay his past to rest? Perhaps Lord Pitt's unconventional methods had some merit after all.

I dragged in a breath, attempting to make my lungs work. "You have no need to persuade me. You are fortunate."

"Or unfortunate." He tore his sights away from me. "Shall we go then, my lady?"

"Lead the way, noble sir." I made my voice light so he wouldn't know just how much his suggestion affected me, how much I liked him, and how much I was looking forward to our time together.

Within the hour, we were on our way with the accompaniment of a small regiment of Aldric's men. I rode in front of him, squeezed into his saddle, his chest against my back, his hand lightly bracing my waist.

I hadn't complained. Secretly, I'd been pleased to be within the confines of his arms. I hadn't even minded the scarf he'd tied over my eyes in his attempt to surprise me with the outing.

We'd ridden only a short distance when he slowed his mount.

My fingers rose to the blindfold, but his hand caught mine, preventing me from adjusting the scarf.

"No peeking," he whispered near my ear, which made my insides flip upside down.

"You are cruel, sir," I responded playfully.

His laughter rumbled against me. And as he lowered my hand, he intertwined his fingers through mine even as he directed his mount to continue on.

As we rode, I was conscious of nothing else but his hand against mine, his strong hold that was still infinitely gentle. Being with him and holding his hand was a special enough outing. I needed no more wooing than that.

Yet, he stopped again soon enough and released my hand to dismount. "Here we are, my lady." He lifted me down before steering me over uneven ground. A short distance away, came the rushing of water, and I guessed we were at some sort of river.

"Will you allow me to see now?" I asked. "Or

am I to spend our entire outing blindfolded?"

"Perhaps I shall leave you blindfolded," he retorted. "Then I may do with you as I please."

"You should know I am not so easily controlled."

His fingers connected with the knot at the back of my head. "You have already taught me that lesson well enough."

I smiled, sure he was remembering all of my attempts at escape during our ride to Tolleymuth. I no longer had any desire to escape this man, and I was quite sure he knew it.

As he loosened the knot, he brushed aside the pretty but sheer veil that covered my elegantly coiled hair. Without the veil, my neck was exposed. I waited breathlessly for his fingers to make contact, for him to graze my skin.

But he finished tugging the scarf loose and made no move to skim my neck.

"Are you ready, my lady?" he asked.

I nodded.

He allowed the scarf to slip away, and I found myself gazing upon the most beautiful scene I'd ever witnessed. Directly ahead, a waterfall cascaded down a hillside and crashed into a rocky river, spraying up with a foamy mist. The thick woodland surrounded the river making it a lush paradise, the summer green of the foliage all the brighter in the glistening drops from the waterfall.

On the riverbank stood a table with two chairs. The table was decorated with a shimmering white tablecloth, silver goblets and plates, along with a crystal vase filled with a vibrant arrangement of wildflowers. Several platters of food were spread, each one heaped with enticing delicacies.

I could only stand speechless at the beauty of the scene.

Aldric stood at my side, taking in my reaction. "Does it sufficiently woo you, my lady?" he finally asked, his tone filled with humor.

"It is a start."

"Just a start?"

I strolled toward the table, attempting to control my wildly thumping heartbeat. The moment was magical. It was more than I ever could have imagined. And it swept me completely off my feet. But I didn't want Aldric to know he could so easily win me over.

He reached the table ahead of me and pulled out my chair with a flourish, helping to seat me before he took the place across the table.

His squires and whatever servants had prepared the table and meal kept a discreet distance away, making me feel as though we were alone in the beautiful wilderness. With the roar of the waterfall as the accompaniment, I could ask for no sweeter music.

Likewise, I could ask for no better company. Aldric conversed easily and engaged me with his wit and knowledge. We lingered over the meal long after we'd finished, the backdrop of the waterfall never ceasing to take my breath away.

With a glance at the sky overhead, Aldric stood and held out his hand to me. "I would make the summer's eve stand still longer if I could, my lady. But since I have no power over the skies, I must finish wooing you before darkness falls."

I smiled and took his outstretched hand. "Finish wooing?"

His dark eyes lit. "Yes, you didn't think this was all I'd planned, did you?"

As I stood, his fingers encircled mine. When I politely began to pull away, he drew my hand deeper into his, lacing his fingers through mine as he had earlier during the ride. As before, the contact affected me more than I wanted him to know. I couldn't deny the threads of warmth that spread up my arm and twined through my heart.

I realized, then, this connection with him would be difficult to cut loose, that his presence was weaving into the tapestry of my life, and that I had no wish to untangle the woven strands any more than I wished to release his hold on my hand.

He guided me through the woodland along the riverbank, seeming to follow an invisible path, one he'd apparently traversed many times in the past. I wasn't sure where he was leading, but I trusted him—more than anyone else I'd known. That thought surprised me, though it shouldn't have. In the weeks I'd known Aldric, he'd proven himself to be a man of great character, one I could trust with my life.

If I could trust him with my very life, could I not also trust him with the mission my father had given me to find the Holy Chalice? Once I explained how sick Charles was and how desperately he needed a miracle, Aldric would forgive me for causing him so much trouble.

"Aldric," I said, tugging him to a stop, knowing I needed to make my confession before I lost the will.

He halted and pivoted. His eyes rounded with something akin to surprise. It took me a minute to realize I'd addressed him by his given name. I wasn't sure if he would accept such intimacy, and I knew I should apologize.

"Yes, Olivia?" he said before I could say more.

At the sound of my given name on his lips, I smiled.

He returned my smile with a beautiful one of his own, one that told me he accepted this new level of friendship in our relationship.

"I would share the truth with you about my crime if you would hear it."

His smile slipped away. Perhaps I shouldn't have brought it up. After all, I didn't want to ruin this lovely evening he'd gone to so much effort to make perfect.

"If you would rather not, I understand."

He closed the distance between us so that he was only a foot away. He lifted his hand and brushed my cheek with his knuckles. "I'd like honesty between us, Olivia."

He spoke my name like a caress, and the tenderness in his eyes broke down any further resistance I might have had. "During the ambush on our way to Tolleymuth, my manservant Cecil passed along my father's instructions to me."

Although Aldric's irises darkened, his expression remained patient and nonjudgmental.

I took a deep breath and continued. "My father learned that Lord Pitt has the Holy Chalice in his possession, and he commanded me to find it for him."

"Why?" The question was hard and demanded the truth.

"My father believes the tales about the chalice's healing power, that whoever places his lips upon the same cup that our Lord used will be healed of any ailment. He hopes it will cure my brother Charles of his illness and prolong his life."

Aldric studied my face, and I did the same to his, wishing I could read his thoughts as easily as he seemed to be reading mine.

"He told me he would not pay the ransom to Lord Pitt until I found the chalice."

"I'm not surprised he would sacrifice you for his own cause. And that makes me detest him more."

"Not for *his* cause. For *Charles*." But even as I protested, I was assailed with doubts. Yes, Father wanted to find a cure for Charles. But I suspected he wanted the chalice because of the prosperity and power it could bring him if the holy relic truly did contain the power it was rumored to have.

Aldric was silent for a long moment, taking in everything I'd revealed to him. Sprinkles of sunlight danced like fireflies in the lengthening shadows, but the light did nothing to illuminate his face and make it more readable. I couldn't tell if he was angry with me. And I prayed he wasn't.

When he reached for my hand and slipped his fingers into mine, pressing his palm against mine, I released a breath. I had no wish to create a rift between us, and I was relieved he still accepted me.

"You must put the chalice out of your mind," he said quietly. "Lord Pitt no longer has it in his possession."

"How can you be certain?"

"Because I have it. Lord Pitt gave it to me, and I have locked it away where it will remain safe."

I watched the shadows flit across his face, and tried to take in his revelation.

"Someday soon," he continued, "after you have become my wife, we will give Charles a chance to drink from the chalice."

He was under no obligation to allow Charles such an opportunity, not after the trouble I'd caused. The prospect was more than generous and showed Aldric to be a man of honor, integrity, as well as benevolence. If I had to bind myself to one of Lord Pitt's knights, I could ask for no better man than this one standing before me.

"I have never met a man as noble and kind as you." My voice wavered with emotion, and I lowered my eyes in embarrassment.

He lifted our intertwined hands until the back of my hand pressed against his mouth. His warm breath and even warmer lips seared my skin, drawing the air from my lungs and forcing my eyes back to his.

As he held my gaze, something inside me crumbled, perhaps my last wall of resistance.

And I realized I had no desire to oppose marriage to this man. I wanted to spend my life with him. Though we were of different stations, and though he might not be able to offer me the status and social connections that a union with Lionel Lacy could provide, I would be much richer in the things that really mattered—like honor, integrity, friendship, and even love.

Was I falling in love with Aldric?

The very possibility made my heart pound at double the speed. I wanted to say something, but the feeling was so new and delicate I dared not voice it yet, even to myself. I needed time to understand and test whether it was real and not just an infatuation of the moment.

At a crackling in the brush behind us, Aldric's body stiffened, and he reached for his dagger, likely without even realizing he'd done so. He lowered my hand and scanned the thick brush and trees around us. Except for the crashing of the waterfall not far away, the woodland was silent.

After a moment, he relaxed and sheathed his knife. "My squires are keeping watch as I instructed," he said wryly. "Perhaps too well."

"You could send them away," I suggested. "After all, I am equal to their strength and skill and can defend myself."

"No, my lady," he said turning and resuming our trek. "They are much needed. Not as a defense against outside forces, but as a protection from within."

"How so?" I asked as I hiked after him.

He was silent for a moment, then replied in a tight voice. "I would defend your honor at all costs, even from myself."

At his answer, I couldn't keep from smiling. I liked knowing he was attracted to me—at least enough that he wanted chaperones.

I was about to tease him for his weakness when we stepped out of the woods and entered directly into a spacious cave that shimmered with a glassy light. The air was damp and cool. And the ground was wet and slick.

Aldric reached for my hand. "Watch your step, my lady."

I held on tightly, though I had no need to since I was nimble and sure-footed. The steady drip of water was rapidly drowned by a loud rushing. Within seconds, I found myself standing in a cavern with water pouring down a wide opening in a steady wall.

"Where are we?" I asked above the roaring. But as soon as the question was out, I'd already guessed. He'd brought me to the backside of the waterfall.

The water was powerful and glorious all at once—the movement swift, the spray cool, and the color iridescent. I watched with awe. When my gaze connected with Aldric's, I could see the awe in his eyes too. We needed no words. Silent reverence was enough.

When finally we moved to leave, the awed silence was a comfortable companion for the ride back to the castle. Not until we reached the door of my tower prison did we finally venture to speak again.

"Goodnight, Olivia," he whispered.

As earlier, the sound of my name falling from his lips sent sweet pleasure wafting through my chest. When he raised my hand to his lips and brushed a feathery kiss across my knuckles, the pleasure rippled out to my limbs, down to my fingers and toes.

"You may tell Lord Pitt you have sufficiently wooed me," I whispered in return.

"Have I now?" he replied as he released my hand. In the torchlight, his eyes were especially dark and murky.

"Yes, you most definitely have."

He hesitated but then seemed to force himself to take a step back. He glanced over his shoulder toward the stairwell. His men were waiting at the bottom. Was he wishing he'd asked them to accompany him? Was he tempted to do more than kiss my hand?

As much as I longed for him to close the distance between us and wrap me in his arms, I respected that he wanted to remain a man of honor. I retreated into the lonely tower room, wanting to aid his intentions toward me.

"It was a beautiful evening," I said, reaching for the door and beginning to close it, "one I shall never forget."

He made no move to stop me. Rather he watched me with an intensity that sent my heart spiraling out of control.

I closed the door and leaned against it. The oaken slab was cool against my hot skin. I listened for his descent, but heard nothing.

Finally, the key rattled in the lock and was followed by his footsteps descending the stone steps. As they faded away, I slid down to the floor, my knees no longer able to support my weight.

I realized with startling clarity that he hadn't needed to lock the tower door, for I wouldn't run away even if given the opportunity. I had no desire to leave him. Not this night. Nor forever-more.

Chapter
17

⁂

"ADMIT IT," PITT SAID AS WE STRODE ACROSS THE BAILEY toward our waiting mounts. "I was right and you were wrong."

"About what, my lord?" I replied, although I knew very well about what.

The July morning had dawned warm and promised to provide sunshine for our hunt. Through the open gatehouse, a mist hovered over the moat and the open field beyond, a vision almost as fair as the waterfall of the previous eve.

I filled my lungs with the scent of damp grass mingling with the wood smoke from the early morning hearth fires. The day brimmed with promise. My heart was lighter than it had been in a very long time, and I anticipated the hunt more than I had any others.

Because of Olivia. But I would not say so to Pitt.

"I was right that you're enamored with Lady

Olivia," Pitt said with a nod in her direction.

She waited near the stables beside my men. Although I would have preferred to fetch her myself, I'd had too many other details to orchestrate in preparation for the hunt. Now as I took her in, my chest swelled with an emotion I didn't dare name.

"She is a fair sight," I conceded.

"She's more than that."

Pitt was right. Olivia was ravishing in the deep purple gown that made her red hair and creamy skin radiate. A belt of golden hoops cinched her waist and matched the fillet that graced her head like a crown, adding to her elegance. A light silk cloak was pinned closed at one shoulder with her mother's brooch.

Pitt stopped abruptly and watched my face, a slow grin transforming his scar and the gruffness of his countenance into delight. "I think you're looking forward to the wedding."

I wanted to keep walking, to ignore his teasing. But I respected him too much to show him any discourtesy. The best I could do was remain silent and, in so doing, refuse to indulge his whims.

His eyes widened. "Saints above, Windsor. You're in love."

"No." The denial fell from my lips too quickly. I realized my mistake as soon as I spoke.

Pitt's laughter boomed around the inner bailey, drawing attention from everyone who'd gathered for the expedition, including Olivia.

I steeled myself with my most severe expression and prayed Pitt wouldn't repeat himself. I didn't want to have this discussion anywhere at any time, much less here in the open where Olivia might hear things she shouldn't.

As Pitt's laughter diminished, he clamped a hand on my shoulder. "Well, it's about time is all I can say."

I shook my head. "You're getting ahead of yourself, my lord."

"I don't think so." He resumed his stride toward our horses. "In fact, maybe I ought to lock her away from you until the wedding."

If he changed his mind about allowing Olivia to go on the hunt, she'd be sorely disappointed. "Have no fear. She's like a sister to me."

"Sister?" Pitt guffawed. "Not in the least. I won't ask any questions if you need to break away from the hunting party from time to time."

I had no doubt Olivia could hear Pitt's statements, and I was too chagrinned to look at her, especially in light of his last insinuation that I'd attempt to get Olivia alone. And for what? So that I could kiss her again?

If I'd wanted to kiss her, I would have done so at the waterfall or even when I'd accompanied her back to the tower.

As it was, I'd resolved to keep our physical contact to a minimum so that I didn't awaken any more desire between us. I was already having difficulty tearing myself away from her. Last night at her door had been pure torture.

"Perhaps it would be best if she rode her own mount," I suggested.

"I stand by my original agreement, Windsor. She rides with you or not at all."

Clearly, he hadn't meant his statement about locking Olivia away until the wedding. He intended to push us together as much as he could to ensure that I would follow through with the wedding.

And would I follow through?

I'd wrestled with that question long into the night, tossing and turning on my bed until my body had been tangled in my coverlet as helplessly as my mind was tangled with how to proceed.

At my approach, my men cast their gazes to the ground. Even so, they couldn't hide their humor or smother their grins quickly enough.

Olivia appeared busy with the bay dogs circling among the mounts, their tails wagging in frenzied excitement and their wet noses bumping anyone who might pay them heed. I could only pray she'd been too distracted to listen to Pitt's embarrassing comments.

"My lady," I said, admiring the gracefulness of her body as she straightened. "Are you ready to commence the hunt?"

"Of course. Very much so." She peered up at me eagerly, her green eyes innocent and wide and beautiful.

I assisted her into the saddle and a moment later took my place behind her.

"Will you allow me a boar spear of my own?" she asked.

"You'll have no need."

"Then you plan to share yours?" She glanced at the special weapon tucked into my sword belt.

There was no way I was letting Olivia get anywhere near a boar. Once the bay hounds chased and cornered the wild pig, the beast would be viciously dangerous. When it began its charge, only the most skilled of the hunters would attempt to make a kill shot. And today, with Olivia on my mount, I had no intention of being in the midst of the fray.

"You must earn the right to use a boar spear," I said.

"How can I earn the right if I am not allowed to have one?"

I should have guessed Olivia wouldn't be content merely watching a boar hunt, that she'd want to participate for herself. She'd already proven she was unconventional and saw no need to be like other ladies. While I appreciated her spirit and determination, everything within me resisted the prospect of her being anywhere near harm's way.

In fact, the more I recollected the way we'd met in her chambers at Ludlow and the realization that I could have killed her, I wasn't sure I ought to encourage her swordplay any further. Yes, I appreciated that she could defend herself in an emergency. But beyond that, I had no wish for her to engage in combat.

Or in a dangerous hunt.

"You must be content to watch, my lady."

"You must trust me," she retorted. "If you teach me, I shall learn the hunt as well as any man."

I urged my steed toward the gatehouse with a force that caused Olivia to lean back into me. Thankfully after only a few minutes of holding herself stiffly, she settled in and relaxed, and for a while we rode in silence. I suspected she'd put the matter of using my boar sword from her mind—at least for now—and had resigned herself to observing the hunt rather than participating.

"It's beautiful," she said taking in the mist, the way the morning sunlight speared the droplets so that bright beams cascaded onto the heathland grass causing the dew to glisten. "Almost as beautiful as the waterfall."

"I was thinking the same."

She curled her hand around mine, which was resting lightly at her waist. At the gentle pressure, I released my tension. We might disagree on her participation in the hunt, but she could let it go for now and simply enjoy being together. I marveled at her ability to do so and vowed to do the same.

"So I am like a sister to you." While the words

had the inflection of a statement, I could hear the question within them, the one asking me to clarify our relationship.

How could I clarify what I didn't understand?

"I was hoping you didn't hear my conversation with Lord Pitt," I admitted.

"It was difficult not to."

"Yes, I suppose so."

She was silent a moment, as though waiting. "Well? Do you view me as a sister?"

I flipped her hand over and let my fingers slide through hers, closing mine slowly but securely. Then I bent toward her neck and let my nose touch her ear before following with my mouth.

She drew in a sharp breath.

"Would I hold you this way if I viewed you as my sister?" I whispered against her ear, taking too much pleasure in the brush of her flesh against mine.

"Good," she whispered back. "I have no wish to be your sister."

I straightened and forced myself to remain in control. On my left flank, Pitt rode his mount, observing me. He would tease me mercilessly this eve during the feasting if I didn't use extreme caution with Olivia. In fact, even if I behaved admirably with Olivia, he'd still tease me.

Nevertheless, I was in for a long day if I didn't bridle my feelings for Olivia. I would fare best if I kept our friendship rather than her beauty at the forefront of my mind.

As we rode deeper into the hardwoods and thick brush, the bay hounds caught the scent of their prey, and we picked up our pace to follow them.

They led us on a wild chase that ended where I thought it would, in a marshy area containing overflow from the river. In the heat of the summer, the wild pigs wallowed in the ponds and marshes and springs to keep cool. Soon enough, we located the hounds, baying at a thick hedge. The leader of the pack lunged into the overgrowth every so often.

At the shouts and excitement of the arriving hunters, the hounds dove deeper into the brush. A moment later, the enraged squeals of the boar rose above the barking. The noblemen among the group dismounted, their boar spears at the ready.

Against me, Olivia tensed. Her hand in mine tightened. And she ceased to breathe.

When the boar burst through the brush, she gasped her excitement. A large grayish brown beast with bristly hair that stood on its back, charged at top speed. The hounds fell away, having done their job and no longer needed.

"The creature is much bigger than I imagined." Olivia's entire body seemed to quiver with anticipation.

Pitt was at the ready and made the killing blow to the creature, stabbing it through its dense hide and thick bones so that it lay lifeless at his feet.

We dismounted to offer congratulations and sip ale that the servants poured, resting in the cool shade and laughing over tales of past escapades. After the break, we climbed upon our horses and once again meandered through the woodland, letting the bay hounds take us where they would. This time, we rode for a while before the bays caught the scent of another boar and began their wild race.

As we galloped hard in an effort to keep up with the dogs, Olivia tossed a smile back at me, her eyes sparkling with the thrill of the chase. "Someday I shall be among the nobility who dismounts for the kill."

At her declaration, all I could picture was a boar charging directly at her, maiming her lovely body, or worse—killing her. A slow, thick dread trickled into my blood and pumped through my veins. I shouldn't have allowed Olivia to come. Once she tasted the blood-pounding thrill of the hunt, she wouldn't be sated until she participated for herself.

I tugged on the reins and slowed my steed, letting the others in our party rumble past us. Several of my squires likewise began to slow, but I waved them ahead. "Go on!" I shouted. "We'll be along."

"What are you doing?" Olivia reached for the reins as though she would take control of the steed and urge it onward again.

But I held the reins fast and brought the steed to a jerking halt.

The braying of the hounds and the galloping of the other hunters began to fade. Olivia turned her excited eyes upon me. "Make haste! Or we shall miss the kill."

I didn't move. "I shouldn't have brought you on the hunt."

"Whatever do you mean?" She twisted in the saddle to get a better look at me. "You know how much I have longed to participate in such a hunt."

"It's too dangerous." I couldn't let her continue. "I'm taking you back to Tolleymuth."

"No. I am perfectly fine and shall finish the hunt."

"I won't allow it."

"And I won't allow you to coddle me."

"This is my decision, Olivia. And we're not staying." I veered my mount in the direction that would take us back to the castle. Before I could dig in my heels and drive the steed forward, Olivia slipped out of my grip and hopped down from the saddle.

She stumbled and fell to the ground, thankfully into a heap of brush. Even so, a spurt of anxiety sent my heart diving into my chest, and I jumped down after her.

"My lady," I said reaching for her arm to assist her to her feet. "Are you hurt?"

Before I could take hold of her, she bounded up

and darted several feet away. She spread her feet, crossed her arms, and glared at me. "I am not fragile and will not break, so stop treating me as though I will."

Was I? I stared at her, the defiant tilt of her chin, the glint in her eyes. Yes, she was a strong and skilled woman, but that knowledge didn't quell my fears. It only spiked them. She was too headstrong and unafraid, and someday that would get her into trouble. I wouldn't sit by and watch that happen. In fact, I loathed the thought of having to watch her get hurt, possibly even mortally.

I'd already had to sit helplessly by as one woman I loved perished, unable to stop the disaster from happening. I wouldn't stand back and let that same thing happen again.

"You are not as invincible as you believe," I stated calmly, taking a step toward her.

"I may not be invincible, but watching a hunt will not bring me harm."

"It'll only incite you all the more to desire to participate. And I won't allow you to join a boar hunt. Not now or in the future."

"Who gives you permission to determine what I may or may not do?"

Again, I took a step toward her, intending to sling her over my shoulder and carry her back to Tolleymuth if I must. "We are betrothed. I'll be your husband in less than two days. You are bound to obey me."

Her eyes narrowed and her nostrils flared with her displeasure. I didn't want to make her unhappy, but I also wanted to keep her safe.

"If you truly intend to marry me," she said in a dangerously low voice, "then you must know I shall not be ordered about like one of your hunting dogs. I would have you weigh my opinions and ideas with as much respect as you give Lord Pitt's."

So she doubted that I intended to marry her? My own doubts had assailed me over the past few days, but I didn't plan to run away from my commitment. Did I?

I shook my head to clear the frustration and confusion from the previous restless night. Even if I followed through, even if we wedded, could I weigh her opinions and ideas the same way I did those of my peers? Most women obeyed their husbands without question. Giselle always had. And Lady Glynnis obeyed Pitt.

"I'm not treating you like a dog," I finally said.

"Out of everything I just said, you chose that as your response?" She huffed and then stomped away. She attempted to be graceful and hold her chin high, but the terrain was littered with windfall and prevented a swift and easy exit.

She'd basically accused me of avoiding the real issues. But what was the heart of the matter? Why was I really upset? Deep inside I suspected my past and all that had happened with Giselle was locking me within a prison I didn't know how to escape.

"Olivia, wait." I gentled my tone and began to

stride after her. I wasn't sure that I was the right man for her, but at the same time, I wasn't ready to lose her. "Please."

At my plea, she stopped. But she didn't turn.

Behind us, the rapid thud of horse hooves told me our moment of privacy was nearly at an end. The pounding belonged to several horses and bore down upon us with an urgency that raised the hairs on the back of my neck.

Something was amiss, though I knew not what.

Olivia, hearing the sound of the horses, finally pivoted. At the widening of her eyes and the fear that flashed there, I guessed the newcomers were not my men returning to chaperone us.

I spun and scanned the woods. I felt the rumble beneath my feet, detected a new scent in the air, and tasted the determination to fend off any threat.

In a fraction of time, I determined that three horses were bearing down on us. I'd already unsheathed both my broadsword and the boar sword. I could fell two men at once. The third would be a challenge, as I would likely have to take out my dagger.

"Aldric!" Olivia called in alarm. "Take care!"

Before I could assess the meaning of her warning, I caught a glimpse of a cudgel seconds before it slammed into the side of my head. The world exploded into a burst of stars and pain. My body crumpled. And all went black.

Chapter
18

"Aldric!" I cried again as he collapsed a half a dozen paces from me. He hit the ground hard, his eyes closed. My heart seized with the fear that he was dead.

To my right the cloaked man who'd thrown the cudgel was bearing directly upon me.

I lunged for Aldric's sword, which had fallen from his grip and lay by his side. I swept it up and at the same moment swung at the incoming rider.

I would have sliced off his arm had he not jerked away and rolled from his horse at the same time. The movement was familiar, one I'd learned during my years of training.

"Cecil?" Even though Aldric's sword was heavier than I was accustomed to, I wrested it back under my control and stepped warily toward the cloaked figure now crouched on the ground.

He sprang up and at the same moment tossed his hood back, revealing his face.

The Moor's bronzed skin and narrow face with the black goatee should have been a welcoming sight. But I was too worried about Aldric.

I retraced my steps and dropped to my knees beside Aldric before gently rolling him to his back. At the warmth of breath coming from his lips and the rise and fall of his chest, I expelled my panic. A rounded knot was forming on his head above his temple, but he had no gash.

Cecil had rendered him unconscious. But I was acquainted with Cecil's skills enough to realize he could have killed Aldric if he'd wanted to. "Why did you choose not to kill him?" I asked, glancing up to see two other riders rapidly approaching.

"Turn him over," Cecil said urgently. "Pretend he's dead and walk away."

The Moor's instructions bewildered me. I couldn't walk away from Aldric, not when he was injured and unconscious. He needed me.

"Make haste," Cecil hissed, tugging me to my feet.

I resisted. "I shall not leave him."

Cecil jerked me closer. "Listen to me, Olivia. If you want to save him, then leave him."

At that moment, my gaze connected with the lead rider pulling alongside us. Underneath the hood of his cloak, I glimpsed auburn hair the same rich hue as my own, a handsome but hard face, and penetrating eyes that belonged to only one man. My father.

He surveyed Aldric's unmoving form. "Is he dead?"

Another rider reined his horse behind my father, a man I recognized as his commander, Sir Eldridge, his strongest knight. He was short and stocky, not an overly large man. However, he was a brute and wielded a heavy hand with his men.

Cecil pushed me away from Aldric. "If he's not dead yet, he will be soon."

Father watched the fallen knight a moment, testing Cecil's words.

A tremor of fear raced through my blood turning me cold even though the day was growing hot. My father clearly wanted Aldric dead. But Cecil had disobeyed the kill order. What could that mean?

I needed to distract my father, take his attention away from Aldric. With a jerk to free myself from Cecil, I approached my father's steed. I lifted my chin and kept my countenance hard and controlled. He despised any sign of weakness and would dismiss me at once if he sensed I was afraid.

"So you finally decided to rescue me," I stated.

"Where is the chalice?" His greeting was as hard as mine. I should have known he'd get straight to the reason for this encounter.

"Lord Pitt does not have it in his possession."

"You are certain of this?"

I nodded. "I searched everywhere and spent three days in the dungeons for breaking into Lord Pitt's treasury."

Father exchanged a glance with Eldridge, a look that told me they'd already been aware of my fate. Apparently Lord Pitt had made sure Father was well apprised of my crime and the ensuing punishment. I had no doubt he also knew of my betrothal to Aldric.

He looked me over as he would a prized possession. "Have they defiled you?"

The blunt question knocked into me, both startling and embarrassing me. But I attempted not to show any emotion. "Of course not. I would have strangled any man who tried."

Father's lips curled into a tight smile that he shared with Eldridge. "I told you she is too tough to allow it."

Eldridge's face remained impassive, his eyes alert. His only response to my father was a nod.

"It is beneficial that you maintained your virtue," Father addressed me. "Lord Clearwater's son would never agree to marry you if he learned you were a tainted woman. I would have had to give him Isabelle instead."

"Isabelle? She is much too young—"

"She's old enough to do her duty to her family if needed."

Duty to family? I swallowed the revulsion rising in my throat. Isabelle was only fifteen and was too sweet to be thrust into political intrigue. She wasn't ready for marriage to a man like Lionel Lacy and probably never would be. She needed someone tender and compassionate who would treat her like the treasure she was. A man too hard would crush her.

"As it is, Clearwater's son prefers you," Father continued. "We shall move forward with the betrothal arrangements as soon as possible—"

"But I am bound to Sir Aldric." After spending the last few weeks with Aldric, I could no longer imagine myself with anyone else. I wasn't so foolish to believe Father would agree to honor my betrothal to Aldric. Yet I was suddenly desperate to find a way to stay with him. "I took vows in front of witnesses."

"You cannot be bound to someone who is dead." Father flicked a disdainful glance at Aldric, but then returned his gaze, this time with narrowed eyes.

"We should be on our way, my lord," Cecil said, looking in the direction that the rest of the hunting party had disappeared. "Sir Aldric's men will return before long."

"He's not dead." Father turned hard eyes upon Cecil. "When you asked to come along, you assured me you could take out Lord Pitt's commander with one blow."

"And I did take him out." Cecil's black eyes didn't waver. He knew how to handle my father better than I.

At the rasp of steel and the glint of Eldridge's dagger, the coldness that had been flowing through my blood pooled around my heart.

I met Cecil's gaze and saw the apology there. He'd attempted to save Aldric, had warned me, had tried to pull me away. But I hadn't heeded him. Now Aldric's death would be my fault. If only I hadn't argued with Aldric and stalked away like a pouting child. If I'd stayed in the saddle with him, my father may have ambushed us, but at least we would have had a chance to fight back together.

The direction of my thoughts took me by surprise, but I had no time to analyze them.

Eldridge slid from his mount. "I'll finish him off, my lord."

Father nodded. "Make it quick."

I was still holding Aldric's sword, and my fingers tightened around the hilt. I couldn't stand back and allow Eldridge to slice open Aldric's throat.

As Eldridge stalked over to Aldric, I stepped

in his path. "You cannot kill him."

Eldridge's expression was one of almost boredom. He began to step around me, but I moved with him, blocking his way.

"We need to keep him alive," I said in my sternest voice.

Eldridge stopped and glanced back at my father, waiting for his cue on how to proceed. I used that moment to bring Aldric's sword down upon Eldridge's dagger, driving it from his hand so that it flew and landed several paces to his side.

Father nodded at Eldridge, all the permission the commander needed to bypass me any way he wished. He unsheathed his sword and knocked mine to the ground in a blow that would have broken bones in my hand if I'd not released it as quickly as I did. As it was, I cradled my hand and bit back a cry of pain even as I bent to retrieve the sword, fully intending to plunge it into Eldridge's back to prevent him from killing Aldric.

"If you kill him," I said, my voice rising in desperation, "you will lose any chance at finding the Holy Chalice."

At my declaration, Eldridge turned and regarded me.

"You said Lord Pitt doesn't have the chalice in his possession." Father's tone was deceptively calm, the tone he used when he was growing angry.

"Lord Pitt no longer has it," I responded. "But Sir Aldric does. Lord Pitt gave him the chalice, and he placed it into hiding for safekeeping."

"And where is his hiding place?"

"He did not divulge such private information. But he assured me he would allow Charles to take a sip from it."

Once again, Father studied my expression.

"If Sir Aldric is alive," I continued, "he can retrieve it and bring it to Charles. I have no doubt he would do so for a good cause. Sir Aldric is a kind man and will not deny us the opportunity to save Charles."

Father remained silent.

As I stared back at my father, another layer of iciness froze around my heart. He'd never shown me any kindness, I realized with startling clarity. Maybe I'd once believed his decisions had been kind, but after living with a truly noble and selfless man like Sir Aldric, the contrast was too much to ignore.

Perhaps my father cared about our family in a general sense. Perhaps he had our family's happiness and success at the heart of everything he did. Perhaps he even cared about the fate of his children.

But he wasn't kind. Not like Aldric.

"Very well. Tie him up." Father adjusted himself in his saddle, preparing to go. "If he knows the location of the chalice as Olivia claims, he may be of some use to us yet."

I wanted to sink to the ground in relief, but instead I forced myself to turn and walk away from Aldric. Though I wanted to insist on tending his wound and riding with him, I'd only put him in more danger if Father suspected how much I'd grown to care about the enemy knight.

As we mounted and rode away, Aldric was still unconscious. Tied and gagged behind Cecil, he had no hope of escape, not with the way Eldridge had bound him. Nevertheless, I'd saved his life for now and had bought myself more time to figure out how to arrange for his release.

"What about Izzy?" I asked when Father and Eldridge led us in the direction opposite Tolleymuth. "We cannot leave without her."

"We do not have time to arrange for her escape this day," Father said.

I slowed my horse's gait. Although Lord Pitt was not as foreboding as I'd once believed, he was still a dangerous man when provoked. Upon news reaching him regarding my getaway and Aldric's capture, he would retaliate. Of that I had no doubt. I suspected he would use Izzy. She would take my place in the game he was playing with my father. And I dreaded the prospect of what he might do to her.

It was one thing for me to agree to a betrothal to Lord Pitt's commander. But it was another thing entirely for Izzy to be subjected to such scheming.

"I will ride into Tolleymuth alone to get her," I said. "With the hunting party gone, I shall make up an excuse that I want Izzy to go hunting with me. The household will be none the wiser until later when Sir Aldric does not return."

My father didn't slow his horse, but instead slapped the riding whip against the beast's flank sending it into a gallop.

"Father, please." I wasn't above begging where Izzy was concerned. "Please let me go after her."

"Leave her." His reply was terse. "She may yet be of some use to us there."

I pursed my lips to keep from blurting any further protest. Aldric's words about my father came back to mock me as they already had at other times: *He seeks to increase his wealth and power in whatever way suits him.*

Was Father using us both to suit himself? Were we dispensable to him? I shook my head and reminded myself we were loyal to one another, that he'd secure Izzy's release eventually.

But this time, even as I assured myself, the words didn't ring true.

Chapter 19

M Y HEAD POUNDED CONTINUOUSLY. I TRIED TO GRAB MY skull to stop the hammer from banging. But I couldn't move my hands.

I wrenched to free myself, but hemp bit into my wrists, awakening me to the realization that my hands were bound. With a swift jerk of my legs, I knew my feet were tied just as securely. And a rag cut deep into my mouth, gagging my throat and drying my tongue.

I opened my eyes to blackness but rapidly acclimated myself to the surroundings using my other senses. The brittle straw against my cheek stunk of mildew and rat droppings. Added to the musty chill in the air and the hollow silence, I guessed I was in a dungeon. But how? And where?

My aching head blurred my memories, and I could only stare unseeingly through the dark as panic settled in my chest. I couldn't remember anything that had happened.

At the echo of voices and the approach of torchlight, I closed my eyes and held myself absolutely still.

Footsteps halted nearby. "He's not awake, my lord." A man spoke without a trace of emotion.

"Then awaken him," came another more distinguished voice. "I cannot wait any longer. Lord Pitt will be here with his forces within the day."

Pitt arriving with his forces? Was he coming after me?

"I can try to awaken Sir Aldric," said a woman.

My heart thudded. Olivia. What was she doing here? A haze of memories swirled through my aching head. We'd been on the boar hunt, but then we'd separated from the rest of the group because I'd wanted to shield Olivia. We'd argued. She'd jumped from the horse. And I'd run after her.

What then?

I scrambled into the far chambers of my mind to find the answer but came upon only darkness.

At the clanking of a key in the cell door, I quickly finished making sense of my predicament. It would appear I'd been injured and captured but Olivia was safe. And if she was safe, that meant my captor was either her father or one of his allies. Pitt had apparently learned of my imprisonment and was amassing forces to come after me and attack our enemy.

The door hinges creaked and boots shuffled in

the hay near my face. One of those boots shoved roughly at my torso in an effort to roll me over. Still I kept my eyes closed and feigned unconsciousness.

"Let me try," Olivia insisted.

"Stand back." The firm voice echoed against the stone walls. "Let Eldridge do his job."

Before I could brace myself, the boot rammed against my stomach with a force that would have doubled me over if I'd been standing.

"No!" Olivia cried out.

At a scuffling and the clank of metal, I opened my eyes to see that Olivia had lunged at the guard who'd kicked me. She'd swung her sword, but the man called Eldridge apparently had quick enough reflexes to meet her blow. And now they stood metal to metal.

From my dazed, slightly dizzy position on the floor, I studied the outline of the guard. With his thick arms and husky build, I could tell he'd soon overpower Olivia.

A frantic need to protect Olivia at all costs surged with a fresh burst of energy. Even though my head was heavy with pain, I swung my legs around, connecting with the back of Eldridge's knees. At the force of my blow, he buckled and fell, freeing Olivia from the dangerous situation.

She jumped in front of me and positioned herself with feet spread and sword at the ready. "Do not hurt him again," she said in a menacing tone.

Eldridge rose from the ground slowly. I was afraid he might rush at her. But he didn't move. Instead he looked toward the older man.

One glance was all I needed to comprehend that the distinguished nobleman was Olivia's father. I'd seen him from a distance once before. Even if I hadn't, the family resemblance was evident, especially the red hair and regal features. He regarded Olivia with narrowed eyes and a calculation that sent a warning clanging through me.

The Earl of Ulster was a schemer. Although he wouldn't allow his man to hurt Olivia—at least not seriously—he would find a way to make her suffer if she didn't do his bidding.

I wanted to caution her, but my tongue was too dry to work past the gag in my mouth.

"I told you I shall ask Sir Aldric about the chalice," she said evenly. "There is no need to harm him for the information."

The Holy Chalice? Was that why the earl had captured me? So he could force me to give him the chalice? Ever since Olivia's revelation regarding her father's desire for the chalice, I'd suspected the earl wanted the chalice for more than just his son. If he gained possession of the relic and started rumors regarding its power, he'd be able to easily sway the masses of poor to his side with promises of healing. Such a following would aid his rebellion against the king.

"You are protecting him," the earl responded.

"He is a good man."

"He's our enemy."

She lifted her chin in defiance. Though I appreciated her defense and kind words, I feared she was only making matters worse for herself. "Let Sir Aldric tell me what he knows about the chalice, and then we shall set him free and thus avoid the confrontation with Lord Pitt."

"You know as well as I do that we cannot free him." The earl nodded at Eldridge in a move of unspoken communication.

"Then you would start a war?" she asked, eyeing Eldridge who had begun to circle around her. She was alert and slowly pivoted with him.

The earl shrugged. "The war is inevitable. Lord Pitt knows I'll not bow my knee to his demands."

I surveyed the cell in an attempt to gain an advantage, some way that I might aid Olivia in her fight against Eldridge. If only I wasn't bound so securely, I might be of more use to her.

"If you start a war with Lord Pitt," Olivia responded, "then you will endanger Isabelle."

"Lord Pitt might keep her captive, but he will not harm her."

Eldridge crept closer to Olivia, his sword pointed at her again. He wouldn't hurt her, I reminded myself. Even so, my blood pulsed hard with the need to free myself, and I struggled against my binding.

Olivia circled behind me to keep Eldridge in her line of vision. Too late, I realized the earl's plan to attack me as soon as Olivia's back was turned. As his blade sliced into the unprotected area of my thigh, I couldn't hold back the grunt of pain. It slipped out through my gag and took Olivia's attention off Eldridge as she glanced over her shoulder at me.

At the sight of her father's sword in my leg and the blood starting to dampen my hose, she pivoted. But before she could bring her sword around and fight her father away, Eldridge grabbed her arm from behind and twisted it hard, forcing her to drop her weapon.

She screamed and fell to her knees.

At the agony in her voice, anger swelled with such force that I began to thrash against my bindings. The tip of the earl's sword dug deeper. A silent admonition cautioned me to lie still or he would cut me so deep I would risk bleeding to death. Then I would be of no help to Olivia.

I forced myself not to move, gritting my teeth against the wretched sting.

"Do not disobey me, Olivia," the earl said in a low tone, "or think of thwarting my plans."

"Allow him to go free, and I shall cooperate in whatever way you command of me."

The earl quickly jabbed his sword into my other thigh. The sharp edge sliced into my flesh enough that it caused me to jerk with burning pain, even as

I held in the involuntary grunt. I realized exactly what the earl was doing. He was more astute than I'd allowed. He'd surmised the situation all too quickly and realized he could control Olivia by hurting me.

"Stop!" she called out, her eyes widening at the fresh blood seeping from the new wound into my garments. "Father, please. Let him go." Her voice was panicked, and her beautiful eyes pleaded with her father.

The earl held his sword above my leg, poised and ready to slice again. The blade was crimson with my blood. He stared at Olivia, as though weighing her suggestion, yet I knew better than to hope he would have mercy. He was too conniving for that. He was also too wise to kill me quite yet. As long as I knew the location to the chalice, I would be of use to him.

"You fancy yourself enamored with Lord Pitt's commander." He finally spoke in a deceptively calm voice.

"I have told you. He is a good man."

Whatever had happened between us over the past month was real and strong and alive. Neither of us could deny our growing feelings for each other. But she would be safer to hide the truth from her father and pretend she cared nothing for me.

"Then if I had not freed you when I did, you would have carried through with Pitt's plans to marry you off to this man?"

"I had to wed him or face the hangman's noose." Her chin lifted again in that defiant way she had about her. Eldridge hadn't released Olivia, but he held her arm behind her back so that if she moved too much she would find herself in excruciating pain again.

"I know you well enough, daughter. You could have figured out a way to free yourself if you'd wanted it." Her father's voice contained accusation.

"Perhaps I decided Sir Aldric would make a more honorable husband than Lionel Lacy."

"Honorable." The earl sneered the word. "And what of loyalty to your family? You would fight for this man rather than your family."

"I would not see an innocent man killed," she retorted.

Her father wiped my blood from his blade and sheathed his sword. He spun and left the cell. When he was in the passageway, he paused. "Be assured, Olivia. I have condemned this man to die. How slowly and painfully will depend upon your cooperation and his."

With that, the earl turned to leave.

Olivia acted with decisive and expert speed. In a move that surprised me as much as Eldridge, she slipped out of his hold, flipped him onto his back, and thrust a dagger against his throat. I tried to reach for the sword inches from my bound hands, but I couldn't make my fingers work. Before I could figure out another way to help Olivia, Eldridge had bucked her, rolled her over, and had her hands pinned to the ground.

She released a frustrated cry that contained her pain at the pressure Eldridge had placed against the tender spot in her wrists.

The earl stopped and looked back at Olivia with something like contempt in his eyes. "Lock her up," he called over his shoulder to Eldridge as he started on his way. "She'll submit eventually."

Eldridge rose, tossed Olivia over his shoulder, and strode from my cell, taking all the weapons and locking the door. Olivia screamed, kicked, and punched. But the stocky soldier didn't waver in his mission. He carried her to the cell across from mine, dropped Olivia to the hay strewn ground, and then stood with one boot against her diaphragm. "Take out your pins."

"No!" She spat at his outstretched hand.

He responded by pressing his heel into her ribs so that she screamed—this time in pain.

"Your pins." Eldridge held his hand steady.

With shaking fingers, she began to tug the pins from her hair and place them into his palm. When she finished, he didn't remove his boot but instead dug it back in. She cried out again and writhed on the floor in agony.

Everything in me burned with the need to slay Eldridge. Yet I was helpless to do anything but watch her suffer, the same way her father had forced her to watch my torment. If only I could take her place . . .

I'd do anything for her, even die for her if I had to. The realization pummeled me.

Pitt was right. I loved Olivia. I couldn't deny it any longer. And just as I'd failed to protect Giselle, I was failing to protect Olivia. If I'd stayed within the confines of the hunting party, perhaps we wouldn't have fallen into the earl's hands. At the very least, if the earl had decided to ambush, I would have had the assistance of my men to protect Olivia.

As it was, I'd put us in a place where we were vulnerable and open to attack. Instead of helping Olivia, my fears had only made matters worse. I thought I was protecting her, but ended up hurting her.

Was that what happened with Giselle too? I let my fears dictate her activities and boundaries. I believed I was doing my duty as her husband in shielding her. Instead I'd confined her too much until she resented me and ran away.

I swallowed my self-loathing. Apparently, I was no different than before. The moment fear ensnared me, I resorted to my old habits. I'd tried to confine Olivia, to restrict her activities in order to keep her safe. But Olivia, unlike Giselle, wouldn't retreat and let me hedge her in. Olivia would fight back, like she had today.

Maybe that's what I needed, a woman who would challenge me, who wouldn't be afraid to tell me the truth when I needed to hear it, and who would sharpen me into a better man. Wasn't that what Pitt said, that I needed a strong woman who I wouldn't intimidate or crush? Was Olivia that woman?

"Give me the rest of the pins, my lady," Eldridge said. "I can't have you picking the lock."

"That is all."

He added pressure against her chest, and I feared he would begin snapping her ribs one at a time. I tried to call out, to draw his attention back to me, but Olivia's scream drowned out my noise.

Eldridge reached down and carefully removed three more pins from her hair before he straightened and exited the cell. He closed the barred door, locked it, and stalked away.

Only after his footsteps were gone did I realize he'd left the wall sconce burning. Dread settled in my stomach because I knew the burning light meant only one thing. He'd be back soon. And when he returned, he'd torture one of us.

I just prayed he'd hurt me and not Olivia.

Chapter
20

I shuddered uncontrollably. With contempt, fear, and anguish. Most of all, I shook because I'd failed Aldric. I'd tried so hard to find a way to save him. I'd hoped by preventing Father and Eldridge from murdering him and by bringing him here to Wigmore, that I'd find a way to secure his release, perhaps even sneak him out of the castle.

But everything had gone horribly wrong.

Hot tears still coursed down my cheeks, tears I hadn't been able to stanch no matter how hard I'd tried, especially as Eldridge had grown more brutal and Aldric hadn't been able to suppress his anguished groans.

With each slap of Eldridge's whip across Aldric's bare back, I'd wanted to beg Aldric to tell Eldridge the location of the Holy Chalice. But Aldric hadn't spoken a word. He knew as well as I did, that the only thing keeping him alive was his knowledge regarding the chalice. Once he disclosed the whereabouts, his life would no longer hold any value to my father.

Finally, Eldridge had wearied and cut Aldric's hands free from the hook on the wall. Aldric had fallen into the hay a quivering and bloody mass. And he hadn't moved since.

I prayed he was unconscious so he'd have blessed relief from his pain. Although I wished I could see him, Eldridge had taken the torch, leaving us in utter darkness.

If I'd loathed my time in Lord Pitt's dungeons, this was ten times worse. I could do nothing to stop Eldridge from torturing Aldric. I knew it was only a matter of time before Eldridge came back. Next time he'd probably torture Aldric more painfully—perhaps bringing the thumbscrews or foot roaster.

Eldridge was experienced enough to realize when he needed to stop and give his prisoners a break so he didn't kill them too soon. He was also patient and would keep working until he extracted the information he wanted.

At a soft moan from Aldric's direction, I scrambled to the bars that separated our cells. "Aldric," I whispered, fresh trails of tears streaking my cheeks. "I never meant for this to happen."

From the scraping of hay, I guessed he was

attempting to sit up. "Don't blame yourself, Olivia," he said in a hoarse whisper.

"If I had stayed on your horse instead of getting down . . ."

"If I had stayed with my men instead of leaving . . ."

We were both silent, letting our regrets settle around us as cold and musty as the air.

"I am overly stubborn and need to listen to reason," I finally said.

"And I am overly protective and need to stop letting fear run its course."

"No, Aldric—"

"I let my fears drive Giselle away," he stated softly.

My protests fell away. If he was ready to share this part of his life with me, I wanted to let him.

"Our families were allies," he continued. "Giselle and I were friends while growing up. She was delicate and lovely, and I thought I could make her love me the same way I did her."

At the thought of Aldric loving Giselle, of talking and laughing with her, of wooing her the way he had me, my heart pinched with jealousy. It was irrational and petty, nonetheless I could not prevent it.

"She tried to love me," he said. "She wanted to. But her feelings never matched mine. The more I tried to make her love me, the more she pulled away. My mother warned me to be patient, but I refused to listen. I thought if we only spent larger amounts of time together, if I tried harder to win her, she'd come to love me."

"You are difficult to resist," I said, hoping to ease his inner turmoil. "Your charm knows no bounds, especially when you nearly kill, capture, and chain a woman to your personage."

"Yes, that kind of charm is very difficult to resist," he said wryly.

"You are even more appealing when you strike a bargain with your master and give your prisoner one week to wed you or face a hangman's noose."

"I'm quite the charmer, am I not?"

"Quite."

Silence settled again. My thoughts filled with Giselle. If I'd been in her position, I would have worked harder to love Aldric in return, not pulled away from him. Even if he'd been overprotective, like he had with me on the boar hunt, he'd meant well and surely would have learned to let go a little at a time.

"We will all make mistakes," I said choosing my words carefully. "Some people ignore their mistakes, too proud and unwilling to accept their faults. Others let their mistakes rule over them with an iron fist, becoming a slave to the past. And still others allow their mistakes to push them to change, letting the past strengthen their choices for the future."

He was quiet.

Had I spoken too forthrightly? As soon as the question entered my mind, I discarded it. If he had opened up to share about his past, then I'd take that as permission to speak candidly in return.

"I'd like to learn from my past mistakes so I don't repeat them," he finally said. "But I fear I am a slow learner."

He expelled a breath that ended in a half-moan that he attempted unsuccessfully to smother. Eldridge had probably broken Aldric's ribs.

The merest remembrance of Aldric's torture sent a shudder through my body again along with burning hatred. With every lash across Aldric's back, my loathing for my father had swelled until it threatened to choke me. "Perhaps I am a slow learner as well in regard to my father."

Aldric didn't contradict me. I hadn't expected him to. He was an honest man and had never attempted to win me with false flattery.

Even so, my words were bitter against my tongue. I hadn't wanted to admit that Aldric had been right about my father's selfishness. I wanted to go on believing that even if I was a daughter and not a son, Father still cared about my well-being, loved our family, and wanted what was best for us. But how could I deny his selfishness any longer? "I have not wanted to think ill of my father, but now I cannot think anything but ill."

Sorrow pushed into my throat, forming a tight lump. I'd hoped my loyalty would cause Father to be proud of me, show him I was worthwhile, make him love me. But he hadn't reciprocated my loyalty or love. I saw the reality now more clearly than ever before. If he loved me, truly loved me, he would have come after me much sooner and would have paid the ransom for my life no matter how much it cost him. Instead, he'd put me in a dangerous situation and hadn't cared about what I was experiencing.

As long as I was available to marry Lionel Lacy and seal an alliance with the marquess, then that's all that mattered. In fact, he'd seen me as dispensable enough to consider forcing Isabelle in my place if I didn't survive.

No, my father didn't love me. And he didn't show any loyalty to me, except for what might benefit himself.

"I'm sorry, Olivia," Aldric replied as though sensing my grief.

"I just wanted him to love me," I said.

"I know."

Our conversation was shortened by the slap

of footsteps on stone and the advancing glow of light. Someone was coming, and I prayed it wasn't Eldridge again. Aldric wouldn't survive any more torture. I'd have to figure out a way to turn Eldridge upon me. Perhaps if I got him to open my cell door, I could try to overpower him again.

I tensed and used the bars to rise to my feet. As the light brightened, I was able to see Aldric and then wished I hadn't. The flesh on his torso was red and raw and bleeding in countless places, including the cuts on his legs where my father had sliced him.

A guard approached with the torch. At the sight of Cecil limping behind him, I sagged with relief that we would have a longer reprieve from Eldridge's torture.

Ignoring Aldric, Cecil approached my cell. He carried a tray which contained a mug along with a piece of coarse bread and a slice of cheese.

"It's all your father would allow," he said as he handed the mug through the bars.

"Give it to Aldric." I pushed the drink back at him. "He needs it more than I do."

Cecil slipped the bread and cheese through my bars too. His diminutive stature and misshapen limbs belied his strength. If he'd wanted to overpower the guards and free me and Aldric, he could have. Something in his eyes warned me against the possibility.

"Your father only permitted me to give you this small meal because I reminded him you must stay strong and healthy for the marquess's son."

I wanted to throw the meal against the wall and send a message back to my father—the message that I no longer planned to marry Lionel Lacy, that I no longer cared about being loyal to our family. How could I be loyal to a man who put his own needs above anyone or anything? Above family. Above the king. Above the country. And perhaps even above God himself.

Loyalty wasn't a birthright. It was earned. And as much as it pained me to think of cutting myself off from Father, I had to stop living my life to please him and earn his favor. Instead, I had to live in allegiance to God and His ways first.

I'd justified my stealing and sneaking and cheating for my family, for Father. But surely true loyalty wouldn't require someone to betray their own integrity. Surely true loyalty showed steadfastness, nobility, and goodness.

I took the meal from Cecil. "I shall eat this meal and shall marry Lionel. But not for Father's sake. I owe him nothing. Rather I shall do it for Izzy so that she will not be required to take my place."

Cecil glanced sideways at the guard who was watching our every move. Another guard stood a dozen paces down the passageway and another a dozen paces beyond him.

Father was taking great precaution with my imprisonment and guarding Aldric and me well. Apparently he hadn't trusted Cecil to come to the dungeons by himself. After Cecil's failure to kill Aldric in the forestland, did he doubt Cecil's faithfulness to him?

I wasn't exactly sure where Cecil stood. He'd been loyal to my father for years. Perhaps my father had sent him down to the dungeons to weasel information from me. On the other hand, I'd always sensed a deep affection from Cecil. As my instructor and trainer, he'd pushed me hard because he'd cared about me, not because he'd been cruel.

"What news have you for me?" I asked cautiously, taking a bite of bread. "Are we surrounded by our enemies?"

Who were my enemies? Had I been wrong in thinking Lord Pitt was the one I needed to fight against?

"Lord Pitt's army arrived a short while ago," Cecil responded, "and now camps outside Wigmore. He sent a message that he wants to have an exchange of prisoners—Sir Aldric for the Lady Isabelle."

My heart sped at the news. Such an exchange

would solve all my problems. Aldric would be safe from my father, and Isabelle would be back with me where I could make sure she was unharmed.

"When will the exchange take place?" I asked.

"At mid-morning."

"And will it prevent war?"

Cecil nodded. Something in his expression informed me that he'd given me the information my father wanted me to hear, but that the truth was much different. Father had already disclosed his intention to torture the information regarding the Holy Chalice from Aldric. He also didn't want my betrothal to Aldric to stand in the way of a union with Lionel.

There was absolutely no way Father would hand Aldric over. He might make a pretense of it, but he'd never go through with it.

Cecil's gaze bore into mine as if to confirm my thoughts.

"Very well," I said, knowing the guards would report our conversation to my father. I had to convince them I believed the exchange of prisoners would happen. "You should have the servants find garments for Sir Aldric. We would not want Lord Pitt to witness his torture. He may decide to attack Wigmore after all."

"You're right," Cecil said as though contemplating my advice. "I'll have the servants locate clothing presentable for him. The master groomsman is the right size. We may find something in his room in the stable."

I nodded, my mind spinning to make any sense of Cecil's strange comment. Why would he use the groomsman's clothing? Why not one of my father's knights?

Cecil bowed, and when he straightened, he held out the silk cloak I'd been wearing during the boar hunt. I'd taken it off when we'd arrived at Wigmore, too distressed to think about much more than Aldric's well-being.

"You'll need this," he said handing it to me.

The closest guard blocked Cecil. "The earl said she wasn't to have anything except the food, and we were to watch her eat it and then leave."

Cecil shrugged off the guard's hand. "The dungeons are cold. Surely you're not so cruel that you would deny her ladyship a measure of comfort?"

The guard glanced at my gown.

I didn't have to pretend to shudder— although not from the cold, but from my memories of when I'd languished in Lord Pitt's dungeons. "If you would not allow me the cloak, then perhaps a blanket?"

"Go get her ladyship a blanket," Cecil ordered the guard.

"We've been instructed not to leave."

"Then once we go up, you'll need to return as soon as possible with a blanket."

The guard hesitated, clearly not wishing to go to the extra work. "Very well," he said after a moment. "Let her have the cloak, but I must make sure nothing is concealed in it first."

Cecil gave an irritated sigh, withdrew the cloak, and then shook it hard like the servants did when airing out bedcovers. The silky material flapped, stirring up straw and dust, but otherwise was empty. "Satisfied?"

The guard nodded.

Cecil handed it through to me, and I took it gratefully.

Then without another word, he turned and hobbled away. I watched him retreat, the guards following on his heels and taking the torchlight with them.

When they were gone, the darkness returned to swarm around me like maggots in a coffin. Aldric had remained silent through the entire exchange. Had he fallen unconscious as he'd done off and on since the beating?

For long moments, I waited, wanting to make sure that indeed we were alone, that my father hadn't sent someone to spy on us. When no sounds were forthcoming, I leaned against the cell bars. "Aldric? Are you awake?"

"Yes."

"I don't think there will be a peaceful

exchange of prisoners, do you?"

"No. Your father will likely lure Lord Pitt and his men into the open field under the guise of negotiating. Then he will strike them down."

"Lord Pitt will surely not be so naïve that he will go out unprepared for treachery."

"He knows nothing of your father's desire for the chalice and will have no reason to think the earl will want to keep me."

I trembled and wrapped my cloak over my shoulders. My fingers grazed my mother's emerald brooch still in the same place I'd secured it before the hunt. "Do you think Father will take you out to the battlefield?"

"Likely a short distance to fool Lord Pitt into believing he's sincere."

"And Lord Pitt will ride out with Isabelle?"

"Of course."

My chest panged with alarm. "Then she will be in the midst of the battle when Father's men attack."

Aldric's silence was enough to confirm my speculations and cause my inner alarm bell to ring frantically. "I have to warn Lord Pitt. Perhaps I can find someone who will deliver a message to him."

"Even if any of your father's knights could sneak away, would any be willing to betray him?"

I tried to remember the many soldiers who

worked for my father. Would any of them do something so risky? Likely not. Even Cecil would be able to lend little help. Father would be watching him with extra care. His trip to the dungeons with the guards had made that clear enough. And Father was likely keeping me locked up until after the skirmish so that I wouldn't interfere.

"At least now we know Eldridge will not be back down to torture you again tonight. Father cannot risk showing you to Lord Pitt if you are half dead."

"I would prefer to lose my life here in this dungeon than have Lord Pitt and my men attacked."

Although I admired Aldric's willingness to sacrifice himself, I wasn't willing to forfeit him. I had to find a way to save him every bit as much as I needed to find a way to warn Lord Pitt about the possible trap.

"I must stop my father." I fingered my mother's brooch absently. But then my hand stilled on the jewel. Eldridge had taken away all my hairpins to prevent me from picking the lock to my cell. But Cecil had just given me a way out—with my brooch pin.

I loosened the back clasp and slid the brooch out of the cloak. The pin wasn't long, but it would work. And Cecil had known it. Had planned it. What else had he planned for me?

As I reached my hands through the bars and probed the cold iron for the keyhole, I attempted to piece together the things Cecil said. He'd spoken of the master groomsman and finding something in the stable. Had he meant for us to take the tunnel that led from the dungeons to the stable? The passageway was rarely used and would be locked along the way. But with the brooch pin, I would be able to work my way through the locks.

However, if we reached the stables and the master groomsman's room, we risked waking him and any stable boys asleep in the vicinity. On the other hand, sneaking through the keep would pose many more risks. The stable was the best option.

I wiggled the pin into the hole, carefully using the sharp tip to find the latch. At a click, I exhaled my relief. "I am free," I whispered.

"How?"

"My brooch on my cloak."

"Then Cecil is aiding your escape."

"And yours." I wasted no time in exiting my cell and crossing the passageway. In the darkness, I skimmed the bars until I located his keyhole.

"This is too dangerous for you, Olivia," he whispered, his voice threaded with anxiety. "I'd rather you stay here where you'll be safe."

I understood his fears now, better than I had

before. Even so, I wouldn't let his fears hold me back. "I am going. And you cannot stop me."

He was silent for a long moment before finally speaking in a resigned voice. "If you must go, then you must leave me here."

"No, I shall not leave without you. We must make our escape together."

"I can hardly move, Olivia. I'll only slow you down."

I stuck the pin inside his lock and began to wiggle it. "I shall help you. And you will be fine."

"If we get caught, your father will find a way to punish you."

"Perhaps he will, but I am willing to take the risk."

"I'm not." His voice contained a finality that set me on edge. "Besides, if we're caught escaping, then we leave Lord Pitt, my men, and *everyone* else with him vulnerable on the morrow."

My wiggling ceased. His emphasis on *everyone* wasn't lost on me. He was referring to Isabelle. "We shall make it out of here just fine." I had no idea how we'd accomplish sneaking out undetected as injured as he was, but I was determined to bring him along.

"You need to warn Lord Pitt. And save Isabelle. You're the only one who can."

Sudden doubts assailed me. How could I do

this? It was dangerous and nearly impossible. But I had to try, didn't I? "When Father discovers I have escaped, he will know I have gone to warn Lord Pitt. What then?"

"Shape the hay into the form of a person and cover it with your cloak. When Eldridge and the other guards come in the morning to get me, they'll think you're asleep. I'll let them know you cried most of the night and fell into an exhausted slumber. They'll be none the wiser."

His urging brought my hand to stillness.

Aldric was right. I had to leave him behind. If I wanted to save Isabelle and Lord Pitt's men, I had no other choice. Even though I loathed the prospect of Aldric languishing here, I had to do the honorable task set before me.

I did as he'd instructed, forming my cloak and then relocking my cell so that hopefully the guards would assume I was still inside. Then I returned to the bars of his cell, wishing I could reach through and hold him again, perhaps for the last time. I wanted to tell him how much I cared for him, that I'd never expected my feelings to develop so quickly, that I would have willingly wed him if given the opportunity.

His labored breathing reminded me of how much he was suffering. I was perhaps the only one who could help him. This might be the last chance to save him. I had to escape and make my way to Lord Pitt, not only for Isabelle, but also for Aldric.

"Aldric," I whispered, unable to keep the longing from my voice.

"Go now," he replied weakly.

"Stay strong," I urged. "I shall find a way to save you."

With that, I started forward, but I felt as though I was leaving my heart behind.

Chapter
21

I brushed aside the tangle of spiderwebs from the hatch and mentally prepared myself for entering the groomsman's room in the stable.

So far, my trek had been mostly easy. I'd had to operate in the dark all along the long passageway leading away from the dungeons, and the lack of light had slowed me down as I'd attempted to work my way through a maze of various locks. My only encounter had been with the rats and spiders.

Now, my quest to escape from Wigmore Castle would grow increasingly more difficult. And I wasn't sure how I would manage. I couldn't very well open the gatehouse and walk through it, not without overpowering the guards on duty or without drawing a great deal of attention from the clanking of the rising gate.

The truth was, escape would have been

difficult under normal circumstances. But with Lord Pitt's army encamped around Wigmore, my father would have even more knights walking the walls, keeping watch for any surprise attacks or unusual movement.

I couldn't let fear stop me now that I'd come this far. Holding my breath, I pushed against the hatch and moved it slowly, attempting to be as silent as I could. When the hatch lifted out of my hands, a tiny yelp escaped before I could stop it.

Hands reached for me and began to pull me up. I thrashed, intending to retreat. But Cecil's whisper stopped me. "Quiet, Olivia."

I ceased my struggle and allowed him to assist me up into the groomsman's room. Although Cecil had no candle or torch, the natural light from the night sky came in through the unshuttered window and allowed me to see the outline of his short but lithe frame.

I didn't know how he'd managed to get the groomsman from his room. From the bawdy laughter outside the stable, I suspected he'd given the man and his stable hands extra ale to distract them.

Without speaking, Cecil dragged my chain mail hauberk over my head. I asked no questions and set to the task of attiring my armor as rapidly as possible. He'd apparently transported it from Ludlow where I'd left it after my fight with Aldric. Like my sword, Cecil had carefully crafted my armor so it not only fit me well but was light enough that it didn't encumber my movements.

When I was finally covered from head to toe, he slid both my sword and dagger into the sheaths at my belt and then draped a long black cloak over me. Only then did he speak. "Stay to the shadows and meet me at the south wall."

As I began to make sense of his plan, I mentally plotted a route through the inner bailey and kitchen gardens that would take me to the meeting place. The inner and outer walls converged at the south, forming a single wall. That particular area was impenetrable from the outside because it was built into a steep cliff that ended in a thick woodland. During their rounds, Father's guards normally didn't bother to check the south wall. They would likely be more alert tonight. Still, it was the safest area for me to remain undetected.

Cecil crawled out the open stable window as silently as a cat hunting for mice. I gave him a minute to disappear into the shadows before I hefted myself upon the window ledge and attempted to be as silent as he'd been.

As soon as I began to wind my way through the castle grounds, I realized the hour was not as late as I'd expected. Although the light in my brother's window showed him to be abed, other lights still glowed in the keep and within the soldiers' barracks.

Cecil had chosen the perfect time for an escape. Most of the knights would be preparing for sleep. Those on watch wouldn't expect any activity from within or without the castle, and few would be outside to see us slithering along the buildings and darting from object to object.

Nevertheless, when I finally reached the south wall, my nerves were stretched as taut as the reins of a runaway steed. I hid in the shadows of the turret stairwell until I caught movement on the first landing. Cecil was motioning to follow him up.

Although my armor clinked with my movement, the cloak Cecil had wrapped around me minimized the sound as well as the glint of metal. When we reached the second story landing, Cecil stopped at the window that overlooked the wall and the cliff below.

"Here," he whispered. "This is where I'll lower you."

The window was narrow, and Aldric wouldn't have been able to pass through it. But I was slender enough, even with my armor, to squeeze outside.

I took off the cloak. Then Cecil harnessed me with one end of a rope before winding and knotting the other through the arrow loop and back around through the window.

"I'll control the rope," he whispered. "You rappel."

I hadn't rappelled much during my training, but Cecil had occasionally had me practice on one of the towers at Ludlow, instructing me on the technique of climbing down a rope while I kept my legs perpendicular to the wall and walked backwards to the bottom.

"Go now." He hefted me into the window. "The guard will be back in a quarter of an hour."

I had so little time. As I slipped outside and positioned myself, anxiety pumped through my blood. I held the rope tight and began my backward crawl. Although I wanted to stop and thank Cecil, I didn't. He wouldn't want me to waste critical time on sentimentalities. Instead, I concentrated on rappelling as quickly as I could while maintaining my balance. His harness held tight, but the rope burned even through my gauntlet gloves.

Soon enough I left the smooth stone of the castle wall and reached the rocky edge of the cliff. By the light of the moon and stars, I maneuvered through the sharp protruding rocks and brush. As I neared the tree line, I breathed out my relief. If a guard walked past on the wall, I would be hidden from view and safe from any arrows he might shoot. Still, I wouldn't feel completely safe until my feet were on the ground, and Cecil had pulled up the rope.

As the thick brush and evergreens worked to hide me, they also took away the faint light that had guided my descent. Before I could find sure footing, I felt the rope catch and then tangle in an outcropping of vines. I struggled for a moment, but realized I couldn't take any more time to free the rope.

I could finish my descent with it tangled, but then Cecil wouldn't be able to pull the rope back up to hide my escape. Not only would the presence of the rope on the wall put his life in danger, but it would ruin the secretiveness of the mission, for surely my father would deduce that someone had left Wigmore to warn Lord Pitt of the treachery.

I wrenched for another moment, hoping to pull the rope free, but it held fast. In the darkness of the woodland, I glanced down but couldn't see the ground to gauge how much further I had to go or if the landing was safe. Nevertheless, I knew what I had to do. I needed to cut the rope above the tangle and then drop the rest of the way.

I pulled myself back up, climbing hand over hand. I grunted with the effort, and sweat beaded on my forehead underneath my helmet. Thankfully, I didn't have to go far before I found the tangle. I unsheathed my dagger and sawed through the rope.

As the last of the hemp strained to hold my

weight, I braced myself for the fall and prayed I wouldn't kill myself in the landing. With a deep breath, I pressed the blade. The rope snapped and sprang upward at the same moment I began my fall.

I attempted to crouch so I would land on my feet and take some of the impact away from the rest of my body. But the ground came too swiftly. I slammed to my back, my head bounced, and my helmet cracked against something hard.

Pain ripped through my body, and then complete darkness took hold and carried me away.

I awoke with a start and sat up only to groan and fall back. I blinked and peered through the branches of the evergreens above me, thankfully shielding me from anyone who might have peered out the south wall tower into the forestland below.

A gentle breeze eased over me, bringing with it the heavy scent of pine and earth. Through the lightly swaying branches overhead, I glimpsed a cloudless blue sky.

For a moment, the silence of the forest and the rustle of the trees brought a sense of peace that made me want to close my eyes and go back to sleep. As my lashes fell, I caught a glimpse of a ray of sunlight breaking through the thick branches.

Sunlight.

My nighttime escape came rushing back, and this time I sat up in a panic. I strained to see past the thick green canopy to the cliff and castle wall far above. The rope was gone. I prayed that meant Cecil had been able to pull it up in time to make his escape.

How long had I been unconscious? What time in the morning was it?

Fighting against the pain ricocheting through my head, I pushed myself to my knees. Nausea rose swiftly and my vision blurred. Underneath my helmet at the back of my head, a warm trail of blood told me I'd sustained a head injury during my fall.

As I forced myself to my feet, I assessed the rest of my body. My left lower arm burned, my hip and thigh were bruised, I'd lost one of my gloves, and my palm was raw from rope burn.

I'd taken serious blows and noted that my head had banged against a log which had likely caused my head injury. But I was alive. If not for my armor, I probably wouldn't have survived the fall.

As it was, the nausea and dizziness swelled. I removed my helmet just in time and retched into the brush. I didn't have time to be sick and dizzy. I had to make my way to Lord Pitt's encampment and warn him to be ready for my father's probable treachery.

What if I was already too late? What if Lord Pitt had left with a contingency of his men to negotiate? What if even now Isabelle was in the fray of battle and Aldric had been dragged back behind the castle walls where Father could continue to torture him?

A sudden urgency propelled me forward.

Please, God, I prayed, *I want to do the right thing this time. I am pledging a loyal heart to You first, to living with honor and integrity, rather than living to please men.*

No matter the cost. No matter the outcome. I was shifting my loyalty.

Hunched and dizzy, I tried to get my bearings. And I forced my legs to carry me in the direction I hoped would lead me to Lord Pitt. Desperately, I prayed I hadn't missed the chance to warn him.

I fought back the pain in my head and arm as I staggered along and stayed under cover of the forest until eventually I made sense of my location. Finally I circled wide so I would be able to approach Lord Pitt from behind and avoid detection from any of Father's guards who might be surveying the landscape from the castle walls or out on patrol in the surrounding area.

When the forestland gave way to open field, I spotted Lord Pitt's encampment. I dropped to my belly and began to crawl, shielding my body as best I could behind shrubs. As I drew nearer, I didn't detect any sounds of battle or fighting. Ahead, I glimpsed some of the knights beginning to mount their horses.

Did that mean I was in time to warn Lord Pitt?

I started to rise, but at the prick of a blade against the exposed back part of my thigh, I froze and hoped my captor was one of Lord Pitt's knights and not Father's.

"If you want to keep your leg, then rise slowly and don't make a sound."

Chapter 22

I SAT UPON MY STEED AND WATCHED THE IRON GATE RISE. It clanked with an ominous rhythm. For a fleeting second, I considered urging my horse into a gallop the instant we could slide under the gate. But with my hands shackled, I wouldn't be able to go far, especially since I was surrounded by a contingency of the earl's knights. With my cuts, bruises, and the broken ribs stabbing me with every breath I took, I wouldn't be able to fight at my optimum and would be easy prey for recapture.

A short while ago, several guards and Cecil had come to the dungeons for me. When he'd approached Olivia's cell, I'd made an excuse that she was asleep and not to bother her. He'd watched the darkened corner for a moment as if testing my words.

Then he'd crossed to my cell and tossed me clean garments. Although I was certain he'd helped orchestrate Olivia's escape, I wasn't confident that he was truly a friend and not a foe. After all, his cudgel had knocked me unconscious and made me the earl's prisoner.

He'd instructed me to get dressed, then allowed the guards to gag and chain me before escorting me to the inner bailey. Now the bright morning light stung my eyes. Cecil had mounted a horse, too, and rode at the rear of the band of knights. The earl, outfitted in his battle armor, was at the forefront, and Eldridge was next to him.

More mounted knights, along with foot soldiers, waited silently in the shadows of the walls, far enough away from the gate that any outsiders looking in wouldn't be able to detect them. Archers, with bows at the ready, crouched upon the parapets above.

My suspicions had been correct. The earl had no intention of conducting a peaceful transfer of prisoners. He planned to attack Pitt and his men at the moment they would least expect it.

Of course Pitt would be wary and prepared for anything. He was too seasoned a warrior to trust a man like the Earl of Ulster. Nevertheless, Pitt would be at a disadvantage against the flying arrows and the onslaught of the earl's waiting army. The earl would be able to weaken and scatter Pitt's smaller army, killing many before Pitt could regroup and counterattack.

During my lucid moments throughout the

night, I'd been able to think of little else but Olivia. I could only pray she made it out of the castle and crossed over to Pitt's camp to warn him without anyone detecting her.

Every part of me had resisted the idea of her undertaking such a dangerous mission. I'd wanted to demand that she stay in her cell where she would be safe. If she submitted to her father and did what he wanted, he wouldn't hurt her. The earl might be calculating and selfish, and he might allow Eldridge to use some physical pressure to bring Olivia under his control, but he'd never torture her. He cared about her in his own way and needed her for the union with the Marquess of Clearwater's son.

Yes, Olivia would have been safe if she stayed in the dungeons until the skirmish with Pitt's men was over. And yes, I'd wanted more than anything to keep her locked away. But I'd forced myself to let her go.

I wasn't sure I'd made the right decision and agonized over it. But I suspected I wouldn't have been able to stop Olivia even if I'd tried. Was this part of the process of learning from my past mistakes?

My fear had caged Giselle—maybe not in a dungeon, but I'd imprisoned her nonetheless. I couldn't do the same with Olivia. In spite of the danger and my overwhelming fear, I had to set her free, even if she sustained harm in the process.

My horse snorted and shied sideways as if it sensed the tension radiating in the air around us. I grabbed onto the pommel, my shackles clattering and impeding my movement. As the earl urged his mount through the gatehouse, I was left with little choice but to follow.

The morning air was already warm, and the whirring of meadow grasshoppers provided a gentle greeting. The sound would soon be drowned by the harshness of battle.

As we rode away from the cool shadows of the fortress walls and into the bright sunlight, I was once again blinded. I squinted to make out Pitt's approaching contingency and attempted to count the number of men.

From what I could see, he'd brought less than a dozen knights with him, and Isabelle rode a short distance back. That could only mean one thing. Olivia hadn't reached him to warn of her father's deception.

My pulse thundered with an onslaught of sudden panic. What had happened to her? I cursed myself for allowing her to go so easily. What if she'd been hurt during her escape? What if one of her father's men had injured her, believing she was the enemy?

I tried to take a deep breath, telling myself I'd done the right thing. But I couldn't manage to draw air into my lungs.

I needed to shout to Pitt and tell him to stay

back. At the very least, I needed to wave my hands at him to retreat. But even if I hadn't been bound and gagged, I was still too far away to make him understand he was riding into a trap.

The earl's knights around me kept a tight formation, likely instructed to usher me back into the castle as soon as the fighting started. If only I could find a way to break free of them.

The jostling of the horse, even at a slow pace, sent pain shooting through my body reminding me of my limitations. I was probably the weakest man on the field, and that galled me since I was accustomed to being the strongest and smartest of warriors.

When the earl was within two dozen paces of Pitt, he reined his horse. The knights around me stopped, hedging me in.

I noticed that Isabelle halted a fair distance away as well. She wore a long veil over her head, and the lacey material hung in front of her face. I didn't understand why her shoulders were slumped and head bent. Was she sad or discouraged? I would have expected her to be relieved she was finally going home. Unless she was aware of Olivia's fate and saddened by it.

Fresh dread hammered through me.

Sir Darien rode on one side of Isabelle. And another knight, one I didn't recognize, rode on the other. Something in the knight's bearing seemed familiar. He was tall and broad-shouldered, but behind his helmet and armor, I couldn't place him.

As Pitt and the Earl of Ulster faced off, they stared at each other, neither speaking. Finally, Pitt urged his horse out in front of his men. With his body rigid and his hand upon the hilt of his sword, he held out a scroll of parchment. "Before we begin the exchange of prisoners, the king demands that you cease all communication and dealings with Lord Clearwater and other Marcher barons. He would have you sign your allegiance to him and him alone."

The earl made no move forward to take the parchment. "You may tell the king I am already loyal."

"Then you will sign this as an offer of your knights and wealth in service to the crown."

The earl hesitated again. "Very well." His voice was hard. As he started toward Pitt, I realized his plan. He would feign interest in signing the parchment but then drive his sword into Pitt as a signal to start the battle.

I tensed. Then I yelled a warning. The gag muted my voice, but enough sound came out that Pitt glanced in my direction. Before I could communicate further, one of the knights next to me slapped the back of his gloved hand across my face.

The pressure split my lip and would have sent me toppling from my horse if I hadn't been hanging onto the pommel. I tried to yell another warning, but the tip of the knight's sword against my throat silenced me so that I had to watch with mounting tension as the earl closed the distance between himself and Pitt.

Pitt extended the scroll. The earl reached for it, but instead of grabbing the parchment, he thrust upward toward Pitt's throat, exposing a long knife he'd hidden somewhere in his armor.

At the thrust, shouts erupted around me and from the castle wall. The snap and whiz of arrows rent the air. The earl's men surged forward to attack. Several of the knights who'd been assigned to guard me, including the one with the blade at my throat, began to maneuver my horse around.

In that moment of defeat, I was surprised Pitt was still atop his steed. I strained to see him over my shoulder only to realize that as the earl had raised his knife, Pitt had apparently anticipated the attack and plunged his own hidden knife into the earl's open vulnerable armpit.

At the same time, an arrow came from well behind Pitt and hit directly into the open spot of the earl's helmet near his collarbone. Several more arrows flew with stunning accuracy, hitting the knights around me, including the one with the sword.

I didn't wait to discover what was happening or who was shooting the arrows. Instead, I used the few seconds to swing my horse around and make my escape. I had no armor and my back was exposed, but I had to take a chance.

The rumbling of horses behind me told me the earl's waiting army was making its advance. But ahead, Pitt's men were also riding forward, clearly prepared for battle. In fact, from what I could surmise, Pitt had strengthened his forces—he had more than just our men fighting with him.

Did his preparedness mean Olivia had reached him after all?

Fresh hope welled up inside.

I glanced over my shoulder to gauge my situation and swerved to miss an arrow. As I pivoted in my saddle, I was surprised to see Isabelle charging into the battle instead of retreating. Sir Darien and the other knight rode alongside her. Why would they do such a thing? They needed to take her back to Pitt's camp where she would be safe.

She unsheathed her sword and pointed it forward in readiness for battle.

At that moment, I realized two things: the tall knight with the broad shoulders was none other than my brother, Sir Bennet, and the woman by his side wasn't Isabelle. It was Olivia.

A deadly chill coursed through my blood. I tried to shout at her to retreat, but again, my gag stifled my words. Olivia had switched places with Isabelle to protect her sister. She'd apparently hoped the veil in combination with ducking her head would keep her identity a secret. Now that the battle was raging, it was clear she planned to take part in my rescue.

Bennet was steering her out of the worst of the melee toward the sidelines all the while fighting off advancing soldiers. Darien was doing the same. But an arrow came flying too closely, missing her head by only a foot.

The chill inside seeped deeper. Suddenly all that mattered was getting to Olivia and shielding her. She was a strong, capable, brave woman. Of that I had no doubt. But she had no place on the battlefield.

At the pounding of hooves behind me, I shot a glance over my shoulder and caught sight of Eldridge riding after me. He'd ushered the earl away from Pitt and had been leading him back to the castle. But now, likely with strict instructions to make sure I didn't get away, he rode low and fast. With every long stride, he closed the distance.

I kicked at my mount's flank. But before I could gain the momentum, pain pierced through my back and into my shoulder. I'd been hit. The slice of the arrowhead, in addition to the pain of my other injuries, was too much to bear. I lost my grip on the pommel and fell from my horse, slamming against the ground with such force that I couldn't breathe.

Chapter 23

Aldric was down and Eldridge was almost upon him.

I shouted another command to my horse, dug in my heels, and flattened my body against the charging beast. I had to get to Aldric. His hands were chained, he was weaponless, and he was too weak to fight. He needed my help.

Unfortunately, Eldridge was closer and reached Aldric first. The stocky commander hopped from his horse and swung the hilt of his sword toward Aldric's head, likely intending to knock him unconscious so he could control him more easily.

Thankfully, Aldric's reflexes were still quick enough that he rolled away. At the sight of the arrow embedded into his shoulder, my blood spurted with new dread.

"He took an arrow to the shoulder," I called

to Sir Bennet, who'd been doing his best to keep me from danger.

From the moment he'd found me sneaking toward Lord Pitt's camp and pricked me with the tip of his sword, I'd seen the resemblance to Aldric in his handsome features. When Lord Pitt had introduced him a short while later as Aldric's brother, I hadn't been surprised.

Apparently as soon as Lord Pitt had discovered that my father captured Aldric, he'd sent news to Sir Bennet. Aldric's brother lived on the family estate at Maidstone Castle, which was in the neighboring vicinity to Lord Pitt.

Sir Bennet had answered the summons with all haste and had brought with him a small army of his own, including a long-time friend, Sir Collin, who was an expert bowman. Added to Lord Pitt's men, they provided a formidable foe. I'd since learned that Sir Bennet and Sir Collin were a part of an elite group of knights trained by the Duke of Rivenshire, the king's brother.

When Sir Bennet had ushered me into Lord Pitt's presence, I'd informed him of all that had transpired since the boar hunt. I'd even revealed to him my father's desire to have the Holy Chalice and his intentions of torturing Aldric to learn the location of the relic.

After I'd shared my news, Lord Pitt had conversed with Sir Bennet and Sir Collin before issuing numerous orders to his men and initiating a plan to counterattack my father. I'd insisted in taking Isabelle's place, and thankfully Lord Pitt had agreed to it without a word of argument.

Now as I raced toward Aldric, I had only one thought in mind—I needed to keep Eldridge from capturing Aldric and dragging him back inside Wigmore. I wouldn't let Father take Aldric hostage again.

Even if Eldridge had overpowered me in the dungeons, I'd find a way to defeat him this time. I was at a disadvantage without my armor, but I'd do anything to protect Aldric.

I loved him. The powerful truth coursed through my body. I no longer had the will to pretend or the strength to deny the love that had been pulsing through my veins with growing intensity so that now it drowned out all else.

Eldridge lifted the blunt end of his sword toward Aldric's head again. I was close enough that I rose in my saddle and leapt from my horse. I crashed against Eldridge and knocked him to the ground hard. I rolled, my skirts tangling. Wrenching them free, I jumped up. Before Eldridge could catch his breath and move, I pounced onto his chest with both feet. Then I pointed my blade against his throat.

"I shall not allow you to hurt Aldric ever again."

Eldridge gasped for breath but stared up at me with his hard, impassive expression.

From the corner of my vision, I saw that Bennet had dismounted next to Aldric and was beginning to cut the binding that gagged him.

"Help him onto my horse," I ordered Bennet even as I moved my boot to Eldridge's arm to prevent him from going after any hidden weapons. "Quickly."

"Is she always this bossy?" Bennet asked Aldric, a hint of humor in his voice.

"Always," Aldric said as he spat the rag from his mouth.

Bennet grabbed Aldric and assisted him to his feet. At the jarring motion, Aldric sucked in a hissing breath.

At the sound of his pain, I glanced at Aldric. Our gazes connected long enough for me to see his fear—the fear that something would happen to me. I could tell he wanted to order me to leave, to retreat somewhere safe.

Instead of doing so, he nodded his thanks for helping to save his life. In that simple nod, I loved him even more. He was a humble and strong man, one humble enough to learn from his past, and one strong enough to break the shackles and move forward.

I started to nod back but felt myself falling from Eldridge. He'd used the moment of my distraction to his advantage. In an instant, our roles were reversed. He flipped me to the ground and stood over me, his boot grinding into my chest and cutting off my breath.

From nearby, Aldric yelled something and Bennet replied. But before I could gather a new strategy, Eldridge swung the hilt of a sword toward my head. The blunt edge slammed into my temple and pain exploded into a thousand bright lights before all went dark.

Chapter 24

THE MOMENT OLIVIA LANDED ON HER BACK AND ELDRIDGE took a swing at her, I roared and barreled forward. I didn't care that I didn't have a weapon or that I was injured with an arrowhead still embedded into my shoulder.

Like an enraged wild boar, I put my head down and tackled Eldridge, taking him down to the ground. The moment our bodies collided, I swung my chained wrists into his head with a strength borne of my desperation and anger. The clank of the metal crunched against his skull.

Even with so heavy a blow, Eldridge fumbled against me, attempting to get a solid grasp of his sword.

I roared again, releasing my anger at him for hurting Olivia. I swung my shackled wrists once more, this time bringing them harder against his head. I pummeled him, until at last he grew still underneath me.

When I finally pushed myself away, my breath came in heaving gasps. The wound in my shoulder burned and blood trickled down my back.

As I stood, I staggered from the pain radiating from every inch of my body, but I searched frantically for Olivia. She lay a dozen paces away with Bennet by her side. He pressed a ripped piece of his tunic against a gash in her head.

I stumbled over and dropped to my knees. Before I could brush him aside, someone had grabbed ahold of my chains and yanked me back to my feet. I started to swing again, enraged that anyone would try to take me away from Olivia.

But at the short dark-skinned Moor, I stopped mid-motion. He started to duck, and I remembered the first sword fight I'd encountered with him in Olivia's chambers at Ludlow the day I captured her. Cecil had fought as well as a young soldier with a surprising dexterity and agility. In my weakened condition, if he wanted to hurt me, he likely already would have.

Instead, he held out a ring of keys and nodded toward my shackles. His eyes held no warmth, but I knew why he was offering to free me. He wanted me to take Olivia away from here, away from her father, and away from the danger.

I held his gaze and offered my shackles.

Blood oozed from a cut in his forehead, and he'd sustained a wound to his arm. But he stuck the key into the lock and twisted regardless of the repercussions both now and in the future. He pried loose the iron bands around my wrists and tossed them to the ground, followed by the keys.

Then for several heartbeats he studied Olivia's face as though memorizing her features. "She'll be happy with you."

Without a goodbye, he spun and limped back toward the melee. From what I could surmise, our men were overpowering the earl's who had begun to retreat toward the castle, taking the battle away from us.

Even so, I wasted no further time. I bent, pushed Bennet aside, and scooped Olivia up into my arms. I began to stalk toward my mount. Although my body protested the movement and weight, I pushed aside my discomfort. I needed to get Olivia away from Wigmore and any chance that her father might send someone after us.

"Let's go," I said to Bennet.

He'd regained his bearing and now stood watching me without moving. He lifted his visor and his eyes reflected surprise.

"Help me get on the horse," I commanded tersely.

Still he didn't budge.

"Now."

"You're in love with the girl."

"She's not a girl. She's the earl's daughter."

Bennet had the audacity to grin.

I would have ridden away with her by myself without Bennet's help if I'd had the strength to lift her into the saddle. But I didn't. I could feel myself weakening. It wouldn't be long before I'd be unconscious too.

"Please, Bennet. Help me." My voice was taut with pain and weakness, so much so Bennet lunged forward.

He reached to take Olivia from me, but I held fast to her. "Help me get into the saddle."

"I'll hold her," he offered, his brows furrowing in his suavely handsome face.

I bumped him away with my elbow. "I've got her."

His eyes, so much like mine, rounded. "Very well."

"Just break the arrow shaft in my shoulder and then assist me up."

Within seconds, I was in the saddle, with Olivia cradled against my chest. The arrow head still burned in my muscle where it was lodged, but with the shaft broken I wouldn't risk it slowing me down.

I turned my eyes away from Wigmore in the direction of a place I'd abandoned long ago, a place with too many painful memories, a place to which I hadn't planned to return.

"Where to?" Bennet asked from his mount next to me.

I urged my horse forward. "Home."

Chapter
25

The softness of a feather mattress embraced me, and cool, clean sheets covered me. I didn't have to open my eyes to know I was in bed. Immediately I sensed I wasn't in my own bed inside Wigmore Castle or even at Ludlow.

Where was I? Had someone returned me to Lord Pitt's?

I sat up and surveyed my surroundings. I was in a large four-poster bed with thick embroidered bed curtains of the richest royal blue. The chamber was enormous with a stone fireplace covering one wall, several long windows along another, and a polished mahogany table with chairs near the hearth.

One of the chairs had been pulled alongside the bed but was empty. A leather-bound book with gilded corners lay on the floor, not upon rushes, but upon a thick patterned rug of the same deep blue as the tapestries.

I slid to the edge of the bed, noting the exquisite nightdress I was wearing with tiny embroidered roses at the scalloped neckline. My hair hung loose in silky waves, as if someone had recently brushed it. I lifted a hand to my nose and caught the fresh scent of lavender and realized I'd been bathed as well.

With a start, I stood, but immediately sat back down as a wave of dizziness overtook me. My head throbbed, and I gently touched the aching spot at my temple. It was still slightly swollen and the gash was tender. But it seemed to be healing.

From outside the long windows, a sweet melody of birdsong entered the room with a cool breeze that belonged to the morning. How long had I been asleep? What had happened to me?

The battle between Lord Pitt and my father came rushing back. I remembered fighting Eldridge away from Aldric, but somehow he'd managed to hit me. After that I knew nothing. What had become of Aldric? Had he escaped?

With a new sense of urgency, I rose to my feet again, this time going slower. Muted voices in the hallway outside the room came through an open crack in the door. Carefully, I made my way across the room until I stood by the door and could hear more clearly.

"Collin has already left," came Bennet's voice. "The Lady Juliana is expecting their first child, and he wanted to make certain he's home for the birth of the babe."

"Then I'll send him a gift with my gratitude." It was Aldric. I released a low breath of relief that he was here. Perhaps he'd been the one sitting by my bedside. He'd obviously stepped away for only a moment, not anticipating that I'd awaken.

"Collin has no wish for a gift," Bennet said. "He's a wealthy man in his own right and has no need of repayment. Such a gesture would only offend him."

Aldric sighed. "Very well."

"He was only glad he could be of service to you and the king."

"Then you will at least allow me to repay you for all your help."

It was Bennet's turn to release a breath of frustration. "You were there for me during my greatest moment of need. And I was there for yours. We help each other, Aldric. That's what family does."

"You're sure you won't reconsider my offer to take Maidstone as your own? You're more suited to it than I am."

I straightened at Aldric's offer. Were we at Maidstone? Their home? I glanced back over the room. It was spacious enough to be the master's chambers.

"You know I love it," Bennet said gently. "But I have Sabine's home now. I have no need for another castle."

The two were silent for a moment, and I considered making my presence known and ceasing my eavesdropping. But Bennet's next words stopped me. "You're the baron, Aldric. It's in your blood. Not mine."

Baron?

Was Aldric a baron? All this time, he'd led me to believe he was a poor landless knight when he'd been a baron?

Frustration flared to life, and I swung open the door.

The two brothers started at the sight of me. I had sights only for Aldric. For a moment, I forgot about my questions and frustration. He was simply too stunning for me to think of anything else. With the half-moon bruise under one eye and the layer of stubble covering his chin and jaw, he was even more ruggedly handsome than I remembered. His dark hair was slicked back and freshly groomed, and he wore a clean white tunic edged with a golden braid, fine hose that defined the muscles in his legs, and tall leather boots.

He was attired casually but in a refined manner that displayed his wealth. And his status as a baron.

"You are a baron?" My voice rang with accusation.

He hesitated and then glanced at Bennet as though seeking help in answering the question. Bennet only shook his head, clearly unwilling to answer for his brother.

Aldric lifted his shoulders and chin and stared back at me. "Yes, I'm Lord Windsor, Baron of Hampton."

"Then why did you lead me to believe you were an untitled knight?"

Bennet's gaze swung back and forth between the two of us, and he backed away. "I think I'll go find my wife and allow the two of you some much needed time to talk."

"Stay," Aldric ordered in a low voice that made Bennet freeze.

"No," I contradicted. "You may go."

Bennet watched us another moment, attempted unsuccessfully to hold back a smile, and then backed away.

Aldric shot him a dark glare as he departed, and Bennet responded with an innocent shrug.

Once Bennet disappeared around the corner, I turned my full attention back upon Aldric.

"You lied to me."

"I didn't lie," Aldric responded. "I chose not to reveal my true identity to any of my men so that I could lead them more effectively. Only Lord Pitt was aware of my true status."

I studied his face, the strong features, the intense expression, the deeply moving eyes.

"You could have told me," I finally replied, the hard edge of my tone softening.

He took a step closer. "Would it have made any difference?" His voice softened too.

"No."

"I'll give up my title if you'd prefer." Another step closed the distance between us so that he was standing in front of me only a breath away. "It means nothing to me."

I was aware of our close proximity, of the magnitude of his presence, of the broadness of his chest.

"You have proven yourself worthy of your title." I suspected he'd renounced it along with his home as self-inflicted punishment for his past mistakes with Giselle. But he'd proven time and again that he would face his fears and be stronger for it. "You have learned from your past mistakes and now must stop punishing yourself for them as well."

His keen eyes seemed to see right through me. For a long moment, he was silent as though contemplating the truth of my statement.

Then he surprised me by lifting his hand to my hair and brushing a long strand off my cheek and tucking it behind my ear. "How did you become so wise, my lady?"

At his merest touch, I melted. I couldn't stay frustrated with him. Maybe he had withheld an important part of himself from me, but he hadn't done so maliciously. Because he'd been bold enough to initiate contact with me, I reached up and let my fingers make a trail across his scratchy unshaven cheek.

At my stroke, his dark blue eyes turned a rich hue that somehow warmed me all the way through to a place deep in my soul.

"Have you brought me to your home, my lord?" I used his proper title, but it was a whisper almost as soft as a caress.

"Yes. We're at Maidstone." He lifted his other hand, started to reach for a strand of my hair on the opposite cheek, but then hovered just out of reach.

I nearly quivered with the need for him to touch me again. I wanted to lean in to his hand, but I waited breathless for his next move. "Am I your prisoner again?"

"Were you ever my prisoner?" He finally let his hand brush the strand of my hair. His fingers caressed the length of it before he tucked it behind my other ear.

The gentleness of his every move embodied who he was—a man of both tenderness and strength.

"If anyone has been a prisoner, it's been me," he said softly. "From the moment I laid eyes on you, you have held me captive."

"Is that so?" My voice was winded with expectation, and delicious warmth pooled in my belly.

"You know it, my lady." His hand slid from my hair to my neck.

I nearly gasped at the touch of his fingers upon my throat, against my wildly beating pulse. His hand spanned around to the back of my neck in an almost possessive manner, one that made my anticipation rise.

"You have my heart now," he whispered. "And it shall be loyal to you forevermore."

I couldn't think to respond. So I said the first thing on my mind. "Then if you are mine, I command you to kiss—"

His lips descended upon mine before I could even finish my sentence. His hand positioned already at the back of my neck brought me against him firmly, letting me know that while I might command his heart, he was still very much in charge.

I lifted on my toes to meet his kiss. The danger of the past days, the knowledge that I'd almost lost him, the delight of being together again—the emotions swirled in a passionate dance as my lips moved against his.

The power of the connection overtook me, and my legs gave way. I broke from him with a gasp and nearly collapsed to the floor. He caught me, his brow furrowing.

"You have the power to weaken me, my lord," I said in an attempt to make light of my weakness.

But he didn't share my mirth. He swept me up, cradling me in his arms. Then he stalked back into the bedroom and crossed to the bed. He lowered me to the mattress and placed me upon it carefully like a cherished treasure. Then he straightened and glared down at me. "If you don't stay in bed, I shall chain you there."

I was breathless and my lips warm from his kiss. I could only stare up at him and smile. "I love you."

If my words took him by surprise, he didn't give it away. Instead, he lowered himself to one knee next to the bed and reached for my hand. "I would carry through with our betrothal, my lady, not out of obligation but out of my desire for you and none other."

My heart pounded a resounding answer. "I would carry through with our betrothal, my lord, not because anyone has forced me to it but because I willingly desire to spend the rest of my life with you."

Only then did he smile, a slow and devastating grin that lit his eyes and made him irresistibly handsome. His smile matched the joyous one that started in my heart and spread all throughout my body.

When he lifted my hand to his lips and brushed a soft kiss on my knuckles, I gave him my heart too. My loyal heart.

Chapter
26

We stood at the front of Maidstone's chapel and recited our vows. I smiled up at the man who was now my husband. And I shuddered to imagine my life without him. I'd almost settled for a loveless marriage because I'd thought it would bring me untold gain.

What I hadn't realized was that a loveless marriage to Lionel Lacy, the next Marquess of Clearwater, might have given me prestige and power and political advantage, but it would have left me empty in the things that really mattered: love, goodness, and integrity.

I'd gained all that and more in Aldric Windsor.

His fingers intertwined with mine as they had many times during the past week while I'd lain abed and he'd sat in the chair by my side recovering from his wounds. Although I'd desired more of his kisses, he'd kept a chaperone in the room with us at all times.

Lady Sabine had kept me company whenever Aldric was absent. I'd taken an immediate liking to the talkative young woman who surprised me with her wealth of knowledge about everything.

I'd also loved Aldric's mother. She was as beautiful and fair and elegant as her sons were handsome. I could see that she'd been a doting mother and was thrilled that Aldric was back home and no longer grieving over Giselle. She'd confided in me how hard the past few years had been for Aldric and was immensely grateful he'd found me.

When I'd finally been strong enough to get out of bed, Aldric had taken me on a tour of his home and introduced me to the many ancient relics and the artwork that had found a protective home within the walls of Maidstone. He was proud of the beautiful items entrusted to his family, one of which was the ring he'd given me at our betrothal, an ancient family heirloom he'd always worn on a chain. He'd explained that his father had given it to him long ago when he'd tasked him with the responsibility of caring for Maidstone's treasures.

Although Aldric had failed to be responsible for a time, he hadn't let his failures destroy him but had let them make him stronger instead. "You're my greatest treasure," he'd whispered to me when he'd explained the significance of the ring. "And though I will likely fail you from time to time, I vow to let my failures only strengthen my love for you."

I'd vowed to do the same.

I didn't ask about the Holy Chalice, and I didn't see it among any of the collections he showed me. Although I longed to try the miracle cup with my brother to see if it would indeed ease his suffering, I'd decided that if I couldn't gain access to the cup honorably, then I had no desire for it.

Upon learning that my father had succumbed to his injuries from the battle with Lord Pitt and had died, I'd been saddened he'd gone to his grave thinking of me as a traitor. But I was relieved that the threat to Aldric's life was gone. All of my father's holdings, titles, and wealth had transferred to Charles.

I'd sent my brother an invitation to attend my wedding. But he hadn't responded, likely too sick. At least I prayed that was it and that he didn't blame me for Father's death. I knew he'd been close with Father and would take his death hard. I consoled myself that Cecil was now with him and would hopefully mentor Charles as well as he had me.

Even without Charles, we had many guests

arrive to Maidstone for the wedding. I glanced around the chapel to see the faces I'd recently met. Of course, Sir Bennet and Lady Sabine were there.

Sir Derrick, Lady Rosemarie, and their infant daughter had ridden from Montfort Castle in Ashby. Along with Collin, Sir Derrick was another one of Bennet's elite knight friends.

Lord Collin wasn't able to attend since his wife was having a baby. But the Duke of Rivenshire had honored us with his presence and had been in a number of meetings with Lord Pitt and Aldric since arriving.

Lord Pitt stood nearby grinning like a proud father. Lady Glynnis, with her colorful head-dress and elaborate jewelry, sat with the other guests, her expression grim, almost sour. As with our betrothal, she clearly had no desire to be present. She'd already declared that she had no intention of staying at Maidstone any longer than necessary.

As the priest finished the final prayer, I met Aldric's gaze and squeezed his hand with the thrill of finally saying our vows. His eyes were warm upon mine and filled with a lifetime of promises.

We followed the guests from the chapel and strolled hand in hand along the passageway that led to the great hall where the servants had been working for days to prepare a magnificent feast. We would have a meal of numerous courses along with entertainment and dancing far into the night.

Aldric seemed in no hurry, and I slowed my steps to his. His eyes took on a calculated gleam that I'd learned meant he was planning something. As the last of the wedding party turned a corner, Aldric opened the nearest door and tugged me inside.

He closed the door quietly so that none of the guests would hear him. And then the moment it was shut, he reached for me and pulled me toward him.

I stumbled against him all too willingly.

"I've been waiting to do this all week," he whispered against my hair as he burrowed his face into the thick strands I'd worn loose with ribbons cascading throughout.

"Do what, my lord?" I asked innocently, even as I wrapped my arms around his waist and pressed against him.

"This." He dipped down and captured my lips in a kiss that was all consuming, one that let me know of his undying love and devotion to me. He took his time, and I relished the sweet meshing of our lips.

When he broke away, he buried his face in my hair again.

"Do we have to go to the feast?" I whispered.

He chuckled and pulled back. His eyes were

alight with love and a happiness that I knew I'd put there. I vowed to spend my life keeping the light in his eyes alive.

"I didn't just bring you in here to kiss you," he said.

"It would be perfectly fine with me if you did." I brushed my fingers across his lips, marveling that now as husband and wife we could kiss whenever it suited us.

As he broke away and walked toward a desk, I realized he'd pulled me into his private study, the place he met with important men like Lord Pitt and the Duke of Rivenshire. He also used the room to house Maidstone's ledgers and take care of business affairs. In the week I'd lived at Maidstone, I'd come to realize Aldric was ready to resume his duties as lord of the manor and had spent a great deal of time poring over the books, acclimating himself to Maidstone's affairs before Bennet left.

"I have a wedding present for you," Aldric said as he rounded his desk.

"A wedding present? It is I who should be giving you a present, a dowry. But I have nothing to bring to our marriage—"

"And we've been over this," he said firmly. "I don't need your family's money."

Before I'd known his true status as a baron, I hadn't considered that a dowry might be an important part of a union as it would have been with the Clearwater family. But as a baron, Aldric could have gained any number of women whose fathers would have paid a large dowry for their daughter's security as a baroness.

"I cannot bestow upon you a gift," I said, "so I cannot accept one from you."

"Not even this?" He held up a cup shaped of a dull but thick silver. It was simple in design, without elegant engravings or markings. But something about it glimmered with an almost ethereal quality. When he slowly turned it, the engraving of the Lamb came into view.

"The Holy Chalice," I breathed the words reverently.

He just smiled.

The cup seemed to beckon me, and I crossed to stand in front of Aldric. I lifted my hand to touch the chalice, but then stopped and took a rapid step back. "I cannot take it from you."

"You're not taking it. I'm giving." With that, he reached for my hand and placed the chalice into it.

It was heavier than I expected. "Thank you, Aldric." I traced a finger around the wide rim and imagined the Lord taking a sip from it. Would it really cure Charles? I knew I could do nothing less than allow Charles the opportunity to test its healing properties.

"Whether it heals your brother or not," Aldric said, "the cup has already brought healing to me."

"How so?" I lifted my eyes to his ruggedly handsome face.

"Without it, Lord Pitt wouldn't have had any way to push us together. Without our betrothal, I wouldn't have had to face my past. And without it, I wouldn't have you now."

He bent and placed a tender kiss upon my lips, one that was all too short. "And who would have thought a woman like you would ever be able to love a man like me? That in itself is the greatest miracle of all."

I smiled. "You are not so difficult to love, my lord."

"Is that so?" He grinned.

I set the chalice onto his desk and lifted my arms to his neck. "Yes, shall I demonstrate?"

He slid his arms around me and drew me close. "Please do," he murmured against my lips.

And I did.

Discussion Questions

1. Olivia realizes she longs for Aldric's admiration because he's a man of honor. She says: "Respect and admiration meant so much more when they came from someone who lived out the qualities." Do you agree with her statement? Why or why not?

2. At first, Olivia justified her sneaking around and stealing because she was helping Charles. Was there a better way for her to get the chalice without resorting to crime?

3. Our culture often tells us that something can't be wrong if we're doing it for the right reasons, especially if our choice won't hurt someone else. What's wrong with this kind of reasoning?

4. Aldric feels as though he failed in his relationship with Giselle, and he's afraid to try a new relationship for fear of failing again. Are there any areas where fear holds you back from trying something new?

5. Olivia says that we will all make mistakes. Some people ignore their mistakes, too proud and unwilling to accept their faults. Others let their mistakes rule over them with an iron fist, becoming a slave to the past. And still others allow their

mistakes to push them to change, letting the past strengthen their choices for the future. How do you handle your mistakes?

6. The definition of loyalty is a sense of duty or allegiance or support to someone. What are ways we show loyalty to our family, schools, sports teams, nation, etc.?

7. Olivia comes to realize that her father was manipulating her for his own desires, that he didn't deserve her loyalty. Is loyalty something you owe someone? Or is it something that is earned?

8. Our ultimate loyalty should lie foremost with God our King. What things or people pull at your loyalty to the King of kings?

9. Aldric and Olivia got into a fight during the boar hunt. Olivia says, "I would have you weigh my opinions and ideas with as much respect as you give Lord Pitt's." Why is it so important in a relationship to give the other's opinions and ideas equal respect? What happens when one person demands to have his or her way without considering the other person?

10. Aldric learned he couldn't control Olivia, that doing so would eventually push her away. Control in a relationship is always dangerous. In what ways can a controlling relationship cause problems?

Jody Hedlund is the bestselling author of multiple novels, including *Love Unexpected, Captured by Love, Rebellious Heart,* and *The Preacher's Bride.* She holds a bachelor's degree from Taylor University and a master's degree from the University of Wisconsin, both in social work. Jody lives in Michigan with her husband and five children. Learn more at JodyHedlund.com

Young Adult Fiction From Jody Hedlund

The Vow

Young Rosemarie finds herself drawn to Thomas, the son of the nearby baron. But just as her feelings begin to grow, a man carrying the Plague interrupts their hunting party. While in forced isolation, Rosemarie begins to contemplate her future—could it include Thomas? Could he be the perfect man to one day rule beside her and oversee her parents' lands?

An Uncertain Choice

Due to her parents' promise at her birth, Lady Rosemarie has been prepared to become a nun on the day she turns eighteen. Then, shortly before her birthday, a friend of her father's enters the kingdom and proclaims her parents' will left a second choice—if Rosemarie can marry before the eve of her eighteenth year, she will be exempt from the ancient vow.

A Daring Sacrifice

In a reverse twist on the Robin Hood story, a young medieval maiden stands up for the rights of the mistreated, stealing from the rich to give to the poor. All the while, she fights against her cruel uncle who has taken over the land that is rightfully hers.

For Love & Honor

Lady Sabine is harboring a skin blemish, one, that if revealed, could cause her to be branded as a witch, put her life in danger, and damage her chances of making a good marriage. After all, what nobleman would want to marry a woman so flawed?

A complete list of my novels can be found at jodyhedlund.com.

Would you like to know when my next book is available? You can sign up for my newsletter, become my friend on Goodreads, like me on Facebook, or follow me on Twitter.

Newsletter: jodyhedlund.com
Goodreads: goodreads.com/author/show/3358829.Jody_Hedlund
Facebook: facebook.com/AuthorJodyHedlund
Twitter: @JodyHedlund

The more reviews a book has, the more likely other readers are to find it. If you have a minute, please leave a rating or review. I appreciate all reviews, whether positive or negative.

Made in the USA
Middletown, DE
06 September 2020